DEVIL IN A
SLEEPING BAG

Scott Honea

Chateau Dumont Publishing

For information, address Chateau Dumont Publishing, 1226 Dumont Dr., Richardson, TX 75080.

www.chateaudumont.net

ISBN: 0692680764

Cover photo by Scott Honea

Back cover photo by Carol Honea

Jacket design by Clay Clayborne

FIRST PAPERBACK EDITION

Printed in the United States of America.

This is where you belong.

Devil in a Sleeping Bag

CHAPTER ONE

Shattering glass and the roar of an unknown collapse briefly made Sam Stone consider that the God he didn't believe in just might be coming through on his promises. If the world was indeed coming to an end, this was news to Sam. His ended eight years ago.

Face down on his bedroom carpet and trapped somewhere between lucidity and a fever dream, Sam lifted his head toward rattling windows and saw a snapped power line spitting and dancing in the sky—a charmed snake gone rogue. The rumbling refused to cease and Sam could hear tree limbs cracking like matchsticks. Self-preservation kicked in at this point, and Sam's instincts told him that if he wanted to survive, he needed to stay the fuck down.

Two minutes later, the forty-year-old stood barefoot in his front yard and squinted at the sun rising above a line of perfectly still palm trees in the distance. His eyes shifted down to his neighbor's yard—Jesus Christ—where it used to be, anyway. In its place now sat a gaping, unwelcome sinkhole, Western Florida's answer to the Grand Canyon. The massive crater stretched from the curb to the house, consuming the porch all the way to the front door. The house itself had been spared by mere inches. In what was left of the driveway, a sonic blue Chrysler PT Cruiser clung to the inside edges of the pit, its rear bumper miraculously hooked on a fallen tree that jutted over the expanse. Two thoughts crossed Sam's mind in this moment; how wonderful the soft, damp grass felt between his toes and that Satan's chasm might have just swallowed his neighbor Sylvia.

Then the screaming started.

Sylvia—a rotund firecracker of a woman, braless in an oversized sleep shirt—appeared at the front door and gaped down at the crater, her eyes as large as the collectible owls she sometimes whittled out of cedar.

"Oh my God! Help! Someone help!" Sylvia screamed, pressing her bulbous face against the glass storm door. She soon spotted her beloved PT Cruiser reenacting the climax of the Sylvester Stallone movie *Cliffhanger*.

"My fucking car! Oh my God! Help!"

As if somehow responding to the voice of its owner, the PT Cruiser sunk one foot further into the abyss. It was like the universe was trying to make up for the mistakes of the Chrysler design department.

"HELP!"

Help seemed like a subjective word at this point. It wasn't that Sam was unwilling to help, he just didn't. He stood and stared, a silent witness to the neighborhood apocalypse. Soon Sam's other neighbors spilled out of their houses. One of them, the Hispanic guy with the motorcycles two doors down, surveyed the scene, raced across the street, and bravely hopped Sylvia's backyard fence. By the time the sun finally surged above the palm trees, he reappeared with Sylvia, helping her traverse the yard along the edges of the sinkhole toward the safety of the street.

As Sylvia and the Hispanic guy collapsed in a heap on the sidewalk, Sam glanced back at his own house, a modest two bedroom bungalow with a banana tree in the back that had yet to produce anything remotely edible. Sam checked his watch, a scratched-up Timex, and considered his next move. It was still too early to go to work, but there was no way he could possibly go back to sleep after all of this.

Sam eventually retreated inside his house, ate three bowls of Apple Jacks, brushed his teeth, and dressed for work. The familiar routine was soothing to Sam after a bizarre and unpredictable morning. He stared into his closet for several seconds, but this was merely a habit. His attire was predetermined: a long-sleeve, blue denim work shirt, a pair of well-worn jeans that seemed to melt onto his long, gangly legs, and the cleanest pair of white sneakers this side of the Keds factory. This wasn't just Sam's work uniform, it was Sam's life uniform.

If a Hollywood stylist were attempting to recreate Sam's look, they would only need to examine the cover of The Beatles' farewell album *Abbey Road*. The guy on the left—some call him George—that's the look. Sam matched it to a T, complete with non-fussed shoulder-length hair and a beard that never seemed to get any longer or shorter.

By the time Sam made it back outside, the imbroglio across the street had intensified. Yellow emergency tape surrounded the sinkhole and Sylvia's house. A pair of EMTs tended to Sylvia, who was shaken but appeared okay. Cop cars lined the street, though most of Florida's finest appeared to be simply standing around not knowing what the fuck to do. Sam glanced up at Sylvia's driveway just in time to see a tow truck pulling the ass end of the PT Cruiser out of the angry ground. For a brief moment, Sam made eye contact with the tow truck driver, who flashed a half-empty stare. "Coulda been you, buddy," his eyes told Sam.

Lost in this exchange, Sam didn't notice his next door neighbor Dennis wander into his yard. Dennis was a self-taught tattoo artist who specialized in tramp stamps in the American Traditional style. He slid next to Sam, his arms folded and his head shaking. "Fuckin' sinkholes, man," Dennis proclaimed. "Third one this spring. It's all this rain, man. Fuckin' ground water. The limestone just melts, and then we got these big fuckin' cavities. The soil just drops, you know what I'm sayin', bro?"

Sam studied Dennis, both surprised and amused that a man with a neck tattoo that read "LOVE IS MY OPIATE" would have such legitimate insight into complex geological matters.

"Anyway, fuck her. She deserved it," Dennis grunted, canceling out his educated insight with a dose of ugly. He spat on the ground, then shuffled back to his own yard.

The sun was blazing now, and Sam departed on foot down the block, away from the madness. The familiar stroll down Sunswept Drive felt different today. Every house had a gathering outside of it—some people Sam rarely saw and some he had never laid eyes on. People with vastly different lives and dreams, all wanting to know the same thing: what the fuck is happening at Sylvia's?

Sam breathed a sigh of relief as he reached the end of the block, but he didn't know why. He stopped for a moment and

5

looked back at the scene, as if seeing things through a wider lens might provide some type of revelation for him. It didn't. It never had.

Sam turned and continued north through the streets of Escapade, Florida, population 6,346.

CHAPTER TWO

With a name like Escapade, one might expect a quiet, sleepy, sun-drenched vacation getaway. But one would be wrong. Escapade was not an idyllic coastal haven where rich East Coast investment bankers came to retire—it was the place where the bath salt-addicted children of those investment bankers came to get high, strip naked and chew the faces off of homeless people. "The armpit of Tampa," it had long been labeled. Escapade billed itself as an oceanside getaway, but in reality, its only waterfront property was a semi-circle of shoddy beach houses lining a man-made lake a half-hour drive from the Gulf of Mexico.

But the tourists came anyway, and they stayed for a few days, or a week. They ate at Red Lobster and they stayed at the Hampton Inn; and sometimes they stayed longer, fueled by

7

some unknown calling—methamphetamines, a false awakening, a woman who made them rethink their failing marriages—or maybe just the feel of salt-free water on their ankles while the sun warmed their back. Each of them had their own reasons, justifications, and secrets.

Sam's route to work took him past the same sights and places every day. Eight years ago—when he appeared seemingly out of nowhere—he noticed the details. Street after street without curbs. Houses built entirely too close for comfort, a covered boat wedged between each of them. Sam once counted the vessels along his path, a grand total of eighty-six in a two-mile stretch. He found it unusual that he never saw anyone actually using them. He chalked it up to the fact that owning a water craft in Escapade must be some kind of prerequisite, or rite of passage. He didn't own one. In fact, he couldn't even swim.

Sam didn't notice the details anymore. He kept his head down and his feet moving, preferring the vertical, swirling patterns of the concrete below to the stomach-churning, sickeningly blue and white wisps of the sky above, and those goddamn palm trees planted everywhere.

Sam waltzed down Campbell Street past Jeff's 99 Cents Store (where he bought toothpaste and other essentials), and then made a right onto Hall Blvd, trudging past the Senior Center with the sign out front that read "Bingo: Mon—Wed—Fri.

Pancakes Saturday." From there it was a straight, calf-burning jaunt two blocks uphill to Memorial Cemetery, an expansive resting ground surrounded by eight-foot wrought iron fences. Escapade appeared ugly up close, but from way out here, the dirt wasn't as easy to see—or perhaps it was just easier to ignore.

Memorial's vast, rolling hills offered a view of the entire city, and further, past its fake coastline, to the real coast—a place that Sam had yet to visit.

Sam's legs were flaring by the time he approached the cemetery entrance, but this was not his final destination. Across the street sat a small wooden frame house with at least a hundred marble and granite headstones ensconced in the front yard. The sign above them read "Dan's Grave Markers, Cash only, No Checks." Sam's lanky legs carried him up a long, narrow sidewalk that split the middle of the yard past an ancient, pole-mounted clock that had been stuck on 2:36 for half a century. With its interminable rows of tombstones, the house stuck out like a sore thumb on an otherwise normal residential street. Some houses displayed Christmas lights year round—Dan perpetually celebrated Halloween instead, directly across the street from the cemetery, like a bail bondsman setting up shop outside of a jail.

9

Sam worked from eight to five, Monday through Saturday (and the occasional Sunday), earning the hefty sum of thirteen dollars an hour, a wage which he had earned for the last eight years of his life without complaint or a single raise. In those eight years, Sam hadn't missed a day of work due to sickness or for any other reason. He was total employee of the month material, if Dan would ever bequeath such an award.

Dan preferred to pay his employees in cash every day, under the table, no questions asked. Sam didn't have a problem with that. He wasn't anti-government or anti-taxes, but hell, an extra twenty cents on the dollar really did add up after time. Dan was sly about it, making sure his employees knew that "technically" they were supposed to report any earnings over $6,000 in the calendar year via a 1099 form—but these mythical forms never showed up come year's end. Just more cash. Bonuses. Hush money, often in the form of Olive Garden gift cards.

Dan was a high-strung, stocky fellow in his forties who always had a cup of coffee in one hand and a steno notebook in the other. He had inherited the business from his father, Dan Sr., after the old man suffered a pulmonary embolism in the front yard at the age of seventy four. For almost an hour after he dropped, people passing by assumed the body that laid face down between the tombstones in the front yard was just another one of Dan Sr.'s tasteless sales tactics.

Sam never met Dan Sr., but he imagined that the apple couldn't have fallen too far from the tree. He pictured senior as slightly more easygoing than junior, but he had no evidence to support this hypothesis. Junior ran a tight ship and often poked his head out the back door to bark orders at his employees. He was a nice enough guy, as long as you were doing your damn job.

The backyard of the house doubled as the "work" area. Granite and marble slabs in various states of completion occupied most of the patchy, dirt-filled yard, and a sun-weathered, six-foot privacy fence ran the entire perimeter of the property. In the back corner of the yard stood Maurice, the "slab cutter," an unflappable African-American man in his sixties operating a large, diamond-bladed cutting machine which sliced giant pieces of igneous rock into tombstones like a butter knife through Wonder Bread. Sam observed Maurice in awe, not only because he was so good at his job, but also because he did it with a lit Swisher Sweet cigar forever dangling between his lips. In their eight-year working relationship, Maurice had never spoken to Sam, but Sam was okay with that, mainly because he was afraid of what Maurice would say if he ever did speak.

Maurice maneuvered a forklift towards Sam's work area and dropped off a fresh granite slab. Sam examined it and gently polished the front with a soft rag until it glimmered. Sam had

11

probably engraved ten thousand tombstones in his time, but he never tired of the look, feel and smell of a fresh slab, a blank canvas.

Sam gathered his tools and went to work. The process was tedious, but Sam refused to rush it. First, he applied a rubber stencil to the front of the stone. After lining it up just right, he slowly and carefully peeled it off. He then used an Exacto knife to peel away the smallest and most stubborn pieces of the stencil. What remained was a perfect outline of the design, in this case, a pearly gate graphic with an angel in the middle. Beneath it, the inscription "Ollie Triumph. April 5, 2013—June 1, 2015. The Angels are singing." Sam took a step back and studied the stone, a bit shell-shocked.

"Two years old," he muttered.

Sam had engraved headstones for children before, but no matter how many he worked on, he had never grown accustomed to it. When he first started, he often thought about the lives of the people whose names he was immortalizing; how they lived, how they loved, how they died. Eventually, the demands of his job wore him down and the jobs and names all began to blend together. He hadn't connected emotionally with a stone in years. His mind simply hadn't wandered into that territory. It was wandering now.

Sam took a deep breath, picked up his trusty mallet and chisel and set out to begin the engraving. It was a meticulous process, but Sam worked with impressive speed and precision. If there was one thing he did well, it was this. Attention to detail and concentration were required in this effort, and Sam had those traits in spades. It was a physically demanding job, so Sam took frequent breaks to step back and get a look at the bigger picture. One fuck up and the stone was toast, and the last thing he needed was a giant chunk of ruined granite coming out of his paycheck. Luckily, that had yet to happen.

After an hour of work, Sam had only the pearly gate and angel graphics left to engrave. Dan stuck his head out the back door and called out to him.

"You done with that Triumph stone?"

Sam stared at his work, briefly lowering his tools.

"Just have to finish the top graphic."

"For Christ's sake, use the sand blaster!"

Sam winced at the thought of it. The sand blaster was loud and unrefined, and any idiot could engrave a headstone with it. Dan loved the sand blaster. It allowed stones to be engraved much more quickly, with a smaller margin for error.

"There's no art in that," Sam rebutted.

"I don't pay you for art, smart ass," Dan retorted. "Family's coming at three o'clock to see it. Get it done." Dan disappeared into the house and Sam checked his Timex. 2:24. He shook his head and reluctantly retrieved the sand blaster.

#

As quitting time rolled around, Dan counted five twenty dollar bills and four ones into Sam's hand. "You do good work, Stone. You just take too damn long. I can't afford to hire another engraver. You gotta start using the damn blaster."

"Did the family like it?" Sam inquired.

"Huh? Yeah. It's fine."

"It wasn't finished."

Dan shrugged. It was finished enough for him. Sam folded up his day's pay and slid the bills into his shirt pocket. "How'd that little boy die?" Sam asked.

Dan glared down at his steno pad, feigning distraction. He was clearly not in the mood to wax poetic. "Come on Sam, we just make the stones."

A phone call took Dan into the other room and Sam watched him go, still curious.

#

A sliver of sun remained in the sky when Sam got off work, and he wasn't in a hurry to get back to the chaos on his street, so he took a short detour to downtown Escapade. The town's center wasn't anything to write home about, but it was quaint enough. Jones Diner sat smack dab in the middle of it all. There

14

are fake fifties diners and then there are diners that have sat unchanged since the fifties. Jones Diner fell into the latter category, and Sam ate there as much as he could. The food and the people were both real.

Sam sat in a booth by the front window and devoured a chicken fried steak with gravy and a large order of onion rings, then washed it down with a large iced tea. After he ate, he sat awhile and stared out the window at downtown Escapade. He had always been a people watcher, and he could easily tell the locals from the tourists, mainly by the amount of desperation in their eyes. Tourists seemed to exude unrealistic amounts of joy, and there simply wasn't enough joy to go around in a place like this. The Bermuda shorts and Hawaiian shirts were also a dead giveaway. Sam had always enjoyed examining people, pinning down their thoughts, and guessing their destinies.

Sam left a twenty dollar bill on the table then ambled across the street to the post office which was about to close. Sam pulled out his remaining eighty dollars and slid the cash into a priority mail envelope. He quickly scribbled a name and address on the front but left only a P.O. Box in the return address location. He got in line and made it to the window just in time to spend his last four dollars on postage. Just prior to closing, Sam snuck down the hall to the P.O. Boxes and found one marked C-11. He pulled his keys from his jeans pocket, found the small

15

silver one, stuck it in the box and unsealed it. It was empty. Disappointed, Sam closed the box and yanked out the key. He exited the post office at exactly closing time.

#

Sam typically enjoyed his walk home from work but he preferred the cooler months to the growing intensity of summer. June had recently arrived and the sun was now clinging to the horizon until nine or later—frustrating to a night owl like Sam who maintained a rigid sleep schedule and aimed to reach his bed by ten o'clock sharp.

Sam felt a growing anxiety as his steps carried him closer to his street. The mental image of the sinkhole had been haunting him all day. By the time he reached his block, Sam could see barriers in the distance. Three orange, plastic roadblocks with yellow reflectors filled the middle of the street. Sam assumed they were there to keep traffic from driving past the sinkhole. He trudged closer, his house within eyeshot now. The activity at the sinkhole site had died down, but there were still a few hard hats and police types hanging around.

Sam stopped as he reached the barricades. An official-looking sign read "DANGER – NO ADMITTANCE." He stood for a moment, unsure of what to do next. He gazed at his house – so close but so far – then spied the sinkhole site in the distance. No one seemed to notice him. His feet and bones ached from an arduous day, and all he wanted was to lay down on his couch and go to sleep. But here he was, caught in this shit show.

Sam snuck around the barriers with as much stealth as he could muster and then slipped through two front yards until he reached his own. He ducked down behind an azalea plant and glanced back at the sinkhole site. No one had seen him, he hoped. His ninja-like movements may have been assisted by his house resting in complete darkness. Luckily, in the insanity of the early morning he had neglected to turn on his porch light. This was a good thing.

Sam entered his house and quietly shut the door behind him. He flipped on the entry light, then turned it back off, thinking the wiser of it. The fact that the electricity was still on at all was a relief. Sam wandered through the living room and entered a dark kitchen. He placed his keys on the counter and opened the refrigerator, retrieving an ice cold can of Tecate beer. Sam retreated to the living room and sat down on a large vinyl sofa. He cracked open the beer, took a long refreshing sip, and exhaled. It had been a fucking day.

Five minutes passed, maybe ten. Maybe an hour. Sam had almost drifted asleep on the sofa when three sharp knocks on the front door woke him. Disoriented, Sam peeled himself off the couch and approached the front door cautiously. He

17

stopped, wondering what would happen if he didn't answer. He considered hiding, or fleeing out the back door. No, Sam thought. This was his fucking house and he had a right to be here. Three more loud knocks shook the house again.

"POLICE DEPARTMENT!" the muffled voice rang out on the other side of the door.

Sam downed the last of his beer and opened the door. On the other side stood a stocky uniformed police officer with the name "Lewis" engraved into a gold-plated name badge. Sam was not impressed by the quality of this engraving.

"Officer Lewis, Escapade Police Department. Are you aware of the situation across the street?"

"Situation?" Sam asked evasively. Lewis handed Sam a bright orange piece of paper embossed with the words "EVACUATION ORDER" in bold black text.

"Did you not see this notice taped to your front door?"

Sam examined the document. "My porch light wasn't on," he said. "I guess I didn't see it."

Officer Fat Face was clearly in no mood for fucking around. "Well, we've got a sinkhole getting ready to swallow up half this neighborhood, and you need to evacuate."

"Evacuate? For how long?"

"Thirty days. City's gotta run some soil tests."

"Thirty days?"

"It's half the street, sir," Officer Dingleberry said, his patience clearly growing thin.

"Where am I supposed to go?"

"Do you have any relatives nearby?"

"No."

"I don't know what to tell you. But you have to leave right now," Lewis demanded.

"Jesus Christ. Can I get a few things?" Sam asked.

Lewis sighed, his contempt for the long-haired hippie in front of him obvious. "Two minutes, I'll wait."

Sam closed the door and turned around in a daze. His eyes darted around the house, trying to decide what to take and what to leave behind. He paced into the living room and his eyes found a stack of records leaning against a bookshelf. He shuffled into his bedroom and flipped on the light. He dug into his closet and produced a tattered red sleeping bag that had served several tours of duty in backyards and camp outs. He grabbed some underwear and socks from a dresser, then three identical, long-sleeve denim work shirts from his closet. He methodically rolled all of these items up into the sleeping bag, creating a sort of fabric calzone. Sam hoisted the bag over his shoulder and scanned the bedroom one last time. An old guitar case leaning against the wall caught his eye. Sam paced through the living room, sleeping bag and guitar case in hand. He spied his vinyl records once more.

Sam stormed from the house with his belongings, maneuvering past Officer Lewis without giving him a second look. The officer twisted around to see Sam slip into the blackness of the yard, past the barricades, and disappear into the dark, muggy Florida night like he had never existed. As his legs found their stride, Sam glanced over his shoulder at the sinkhole in Sylvia's yard. Lit by a single, bug-swarmed streetlamp, the pit loomed darker and deeper than ever, like some goddamn portal to Hell. In that brief moment, Sam became convinced that the crevasse had opened for a reason, and that it had meant to swallow him. It was quite a revelation for someone who absolutely, unequivocally did not believe in fate.

CHAPTER THREE

Squinting through slumber and the blinding early morning sunlight, Sam mistook the figure in the doorway for a civil war soldier, and for a moment he fully accepted that he was in the
presence of a ghost. He was in a mausoleum, after all, and for all
he knew the war between the north and the south might have
stretched as far south as Florida, though he had no historical
knowledge to back this up.

As the sleep worked its way to the corners of Sam's eyes,
the soldier came into full view and slowly transitioned into an
older Hispanic man with a vacuum cleaner and a name tag that
read "Jesus." Sam peeled his face off the maroon, industrial-
quality carpet and made eye contact with his lord and savior.
Jesus could only stare fearfully—no doubt befuddled as to why

21

there was a man lying face down in a locked catacomb where bodies were stacked five high, enclosed in the finest marble southern Florida could import from Indiana. A bead of sweat lifted on Jesus' face as he took a step backwards, retracting and rewrapping the vacuum cleaner power cord as quickly as he could.

"Sorry," Jesus sputtered.

"Hey man, no, it's okay," Sam pleaded, but it was too late, Jesus had hightailed it the fuck out of Dodge. Sam sat up, completely unaware that the swirled pattern in the carpet had transferred onto the left side of his face and he now resembled some kind of hippie tribal warrior.

It took Sam a minute to figure out where he was, why he was there, and what had happened the night before. He scanned the mausoleum and let out a sigh of relief at the sight of his few belongings scattered about. His sleeping bag rested neatly against the vault that held Helen Price (1910-1974). His guitar case sat next to it, leaning against the final resting place of Harmon K. Walden (1919-2005). Below it, a copy of Willie Nelson's "Shotgun Willie" album stared back from the tomb of Harmon's wife Wanda (1923-2007).

Sam quickly gathered his items and exited the mausoleum, desperate to find a place to take his morning piss. He only made it five feet before the cemetery manager, Greg, hopped out of his shiny new Ford F-150 and approached Sam wearing a toothpaste-white, embroidered dress shirt tucked into starched Wranglers.

"Hey. What do you think you're doing?" Greg asked, chomping on a piece of gum as though he were a member of the competitive gum chomper's society.

"Leaving," Sam rebutted, moving as quickly as he could away from the mausoleum.

"How did you get in there?"

"The door was unlocked."

"No. It wasn't."

"Alright," Sam conceded.

"That door is locked at eight o'clock, nightly."

Sam trudged forward, ignoring Greg.

"Where do you think you're going?" Greg called out.

"To work."

"Well you can't just … hey!" Greg shouted, backtracking toward his truck. Sam was about fifty feet deep into the cemetery by now as Greg stood and stared.

"Fucking vagrant," he said, glancing at Jesus, who could do nothing but shrug.

It took Sam exactly nine minutes to walk from the mausoleum to work, and another three to expel the urine from his bladder in the bathroom that employees weren't technically supposed to use. But these were rare circumstances, and besides, the boss wouldn't be arriving for another couple of hours.

Sam wandered into the backyard and stood on the porch, glaring east toward the rising run. For five solid minutes, Sam allowed himself to enjoy the peace and quiet of the morning, but this moment of reflection would be fleeting, as Maurice's old Chevy truck soon rumbled up the driveway.

#

With only two tombstones to complete in his shift, Sam's day dragged. Dan rolled in at noon, stormed into the back and demanded to know who in the hell's stuff was clogging up the storage closet. Sam claimed the loot and told Dan about the sinkhole and the evacuation, but Dan's main concern remained getting Sam's belongings out of his storage closet. Sam didn't believe that Dan intended to be an asshole, it was just ingrained in him.

Around three o'clock, Dan instructed Sam and Maurice to take the rest of the day off. Sam waited as Dan paid Maurice for the day, giving him a full day's pay despite leaving two hours early. Sam thought this was incredibly gracious of Dan, but soon discovered that his own pay would not reflect this same generosity. Sam felt slighted, but Maurice had worked there something like 180 years, and there was something to be said for that kind of loyalty. Sam didn't mind leaving early—he now had two

24

extra hours to figure out wherever the hell he was going to stay tonight. The seventy-eight dollars cash in his shirt pocket didn't hurt either.

Sam exited Dan's through the front entrance and found a familiar sight moving through the street in front of him – a funeral procession. At least twenty-five cars, maybe fifty, drove one by one into the cemetery entrance. Sam reacted as he always did in these situations, stopping and watching out of respect. The processions always followed the same pattern: two motorcycle cops, the hearse, the car with the pallbearers, then the family. Sam peered into one of the family cars, a white stretch limo, and made brief eye contact with a distraught woman in her early thirties. The moment lasted only a few seconds, but when it ended, Sam felt an ineffable sadness consume him.

After the final car turned into the cemetery, Sam did something he had never done before—he joined the procession on foot. He walked into the cemetery and set his belongings down behind an old oak tree. A makeshift tent with a funeral home logo kept the grieving family in shade. Additional mourners stretched out into the sun, five rows deep. Behind them sat a backhoe where two gravediggers smoked cigarettes and thumped their watches, making no attempt at inconspicuousness. Sam found this to be disrespectful, but he understood that they were just there to do a job.

After half an hour or so the funeral drew to a close. The mourners hugged, trickled away from the fresh hole in the ground and found their cars. They then shut their doors, cranked their engines, and exited the cemetery back into the world of the living where there were bills to pay and dinners to decide upon. Only one mourner remained—the woman from the procession whose anguish had torn a hole in Sam. He watched her linger at the grave for a moment, keeping his distance. With no water left in her eyes, she finally departed, leaving only Sam and the gravediggers, who lowered the casket and covered it in dirt. When they left, all that remained was a mound of earth arching out of the ground like a colossal anthill.

Sam had no idea why he had stayed so long, leaning against that tree. The two hours of free time Dan had so graciously given him were gone, but not wasted. He still didn't know where he was going to stay that night, but he was certain it wasn't going to be in the mausoleum again. Before leaving, Sam decided to visit the fresh grave and pay his own respects. The ramble took two minutes as Sam approached and delicately stepped around the gravestone. That's when he saw it.

"Ollie Triumph. April 5, 2013—June 1, 2015. The Angels are singing," etched into granite by his own hands. Sam felt a melancholy grow inside him that hadn't manifested in years. The only thing that kept him from breaking on the spot was the shoddy, rushed pearly gate graphic centered at the top of the tombstone. Sam winced at it. He knew he could've done a better job if Dan had given him more time. Sam shook his head and collected his belongings, collecting his guitar and records, and the sleeping bag that dug into his shoulder the entire two-mile walk to the Super 8 Motel.

#

Sam pulled three twenty-dollar bills from his shirt pocket and slid them underneath an acrylic booth window outside a white, two-level motel with orange doors.

"Is this enough for two nights?" Sam inquired.

The man on the inside of the booth moved a creaky, metal 1970's-era microphone to his chapped lips and produced a clipboard from his desk while gripping a stolen Putt Putt golf pencil with his fat fingers.

"License plate number," the ogre breathed into the microphone.

"I don't have a car," Sam said.

The ogre let out a deep sigh into the microphone that sent ripples of distortion through the broken speaker on the outside. After what felt like an eternity, a brass key slid back out through the window. Before Sam could say anything else, the ogre turned off the microphone and picked up the issue of Field &

Stream he had been perusing before this exhausting transaction completely fucked up his day.

Sam trudged up a flight of concrete stairs and found his room at the end of the hall – Room 212. Sam turned the key, opened the door, and dragged his belongings inside.

CHAPTER FOUR

With its buzzing lights, clanging lockers and noisy vending machines, the doctors' break room wasn't much of a place to sleep, but Alan Walker was trying. As he lay flat on his back on a rigid locker bench, the rest he so desperately craved continued to elude him. Unable to drift, Alan focused on the electricity in his fingertips that shot up his arms to his shoulders and neck, his nervous system's response to so many sleepless hours in this frantic dungeon.

Alan hadn't slept in almost forty-eight hours. This wasn't out of the ordinary for the first-year surgical resident at Houston's St. John's Hospital, but the fatigue was especially draining tonight. Twenty hours into a sixteen-hour shift, Alan sought rest in the doctor's lounge after a particularly stressful battle with a

29

nine-millimeter bullet lodged in the shoulder of a fifteen-year-old high school student. The surgery had been a success and the patient had survived, but as Alan stared up at a buzzing fluorescent light on the ceiling above, he questioned whether he was truly cut out for emergency room trauma. He had only been out of medical school for three years, and the emotional toll was already beginning to mount.

Becoming an emergency room surgeon wasn't Alan's chosen career path, it was just where he had ended up. While his fellow students all found their specialties and pushed toward them with vigor, Alan never found a specific area of medicine that thrilled him, but he pursued surgery anyway. He found the track to becoming a heart or brain surgeon both intimidating and time-consuming, and he didn't want to wait until he was forty to start making a difference—he wanted to make a difference now. And so, Alan decided in his final year at medical school that trauma would be his chosen field.

Driven less by humanitarianism and more by a desperate need to pay his student loans, Alan took an internship at a county-run hospital in the most economically disadvantaged neighborhood inside Houston's 610 Loop. Near the heart of downtown's third ward, St. John's Hospital was the kind of place where people came to die more often than they came to get well. Gang shootings were an everyday occurrence, as were drug overdoses and back alley abortions gone wrong. It had been nine months since Hurricane Katrina, and Houston had seen an influx of refugees from New Orleans, all looking for a place to start over. As the inner city swelled, so did crime, and so did St. John's. Like busted levees, St. John's was almost always overflowing.

Alan was damn good at what he did for a living. His hands possessed an uncanny agility with fingers that could weave, cut and stitch with a level of detail normally reserved for much more experienced surgeons. It drew the ire of a few of them, and they often made it their mission to push and test him whenever possible. Alan loved the guidance, but hated the competitive side of it all. More than anything, he just wanted to help people, but right now all he really wanted was ten minutes of sleep.

Alan finally drifted into that strange nether world between sleep and consciousness, and briefly had an out of body experience where he found himself standing at a vending machine trying to choose between a Snickers and a Mr. Goodbar. He glanced over his shoulder and saw his own body lying down on that uncomfortable bench – a hallucination staring back at him - then stuck five quarters into the machine and clicked A7.

A Mr. Goodbar fell from the top rack.

Alan's eyes jolted open as he realized he was not at the vending machine nor did he possess a candy bar. Delirium was taking hold. Alan stumbled to the sink to wash his face. His aching legs carried his tall frame to the basin, where he splashed a generous amount of water across his sturdy, boyish face. Alan rubbed his hands along his chin. Normally clean-cut, he now sported two days worth of stubble, which was both uncomfortable and uncharacteristic.

Alan stepped back from the sink and glared down at his once white tennis shoes, which were now dotted with splashes of dried blood. Even the protective socks he wore over his shoes in surgery hadn't kept a miniature Jackson Pollock from sneaking into the operating room and turning his Nikes into a canvas. He pictured the tiny, miniaturized artist standing on his shoes with his arms spread wide as the blood rained down.

Anger set in at this point. Not about the shoes, but about the doctor who had called in sick and created this whole mess. Alan should have been off hours ago. He'd done his time, but because Dr. Moorpark's ten-year-old daughter had a school play or mono or whatever it fucking was, Alan remained, unraveling as the minutes ticked by. Alan suddenly realized that in the madness of the last few hours he hadn't even called to cancel some important plans.

"Fuck," Alan heaved, running to the phone in the lounge and punching in the numbers. "Hey, it's me," he said into the phone. "I'm so sorry. I'm late. I know. I'm going to make this up to you. I should be out of here in an hour, two at the most." Alan hung up the phone and let out a deep sigh. His pager suddenly flashed. He retrieved it and spied the number, "1214—SR 2."

"Are you fucking kidding me?"

Alan Walker—exhausted, angry, and barely clinging to his sanity—was being called back into surgery.

CHAPTER FIVE

It had been years since Sam had slept in a motel, and his normally reliable natural alarm clock wasn't ticking as accurately in this new environment. The red LED on the night stand next to the bed couldn't possibly say 9:22. Not 9:22 a.m., anyway. Sam flew out of bed, threw open the vinyl blackout curtains and squinted like a vampire at the wall of sunlight that came flooding into the room.

He raced to work, a sprint through a swampy hell—temperatures already peeling paint at ninety degrees. By the time he arrived at work, almost two hours late, Sam was a certified sweatbox, but there was no time to clean up or even catch his breath. He patrolled the house trying to find Dan, but he was missing in action. Thank God. Sam had dodged a bullet, or so he thought. Sam slipped into the backyard and discovered something he had never witnessed before – Dan sandblasting the shit out of a granite stone. This was not going to end well.

"You're two fucking hours late!" Dan yelled over the impossibly loud vibrations of sand grinding away stone. The blasting finally stopped.

"I'm so sorry. I overslept," Sam confessed.

Dan dropped the sandblaster to the ground and stormed around the side of the tombstone. "You know how much I get paid to do your job?"

Sam stared blankly.

"Nothing," Dan continued, because I have my own job to do."

"I know," Sam said.

"So get over here and do your job!"

Sam complied, retrieving the sandblaster from the ground and peering at a half-finished marker with the name "Gerald M. Leonar," still lacking the "d" to complete his last name.

Dan huffed back inside and slammed the sliding glass door. Sam looked up at Maurice, who stared back blankly with a half-smoked Swisher Sweet between his lips. Sam shook his head, more angry at himself than anything. The last thing he needed, after temporarily losing his house, was to lose his job.

#

Sam employed the sand blaster for the remainder of his shift, knowing full well that today was not the day to argue with Dan. It was a losing battle anyway—Sam had seen the brochures and catalogs in Dan's office. Forget hand etching, even sand blasting would go the way of the dodo if Dan ordered one of those fancy new automated laser cutters that could etch a face, script or anything else onto pure black granite in seconds flat. But they were pricy, and Sam knew how cheap Dan was, so he held his concerns at bay.

After finishing his last stone of the day, Sam received his docked pay from a still sore Dan and traipsed into the backyard, slipping a chisel and mallet into his back pocket. He then trekked across the street into the cemetery, on a mission.

#

Determined to put in a full day's work, Sam set chisel to stone and began to chip away at the pearly gates on Ollie Triumph's tombstone. Daylight was precious and Sam desperately wanted to finish the stone before nightfall. The details started to fill in and after half an hour of hustling, Sam took a short break to rest his fatigued hands. He stepped back and examined the stone, picking out the spaces that still needed more detail.

"What do you think you're doing?" a voice called out from behind. Sam spun around to find a woman in a pair of old jeans and a Jimmy Buffett tour t-shirt from 1982 staring back at him.

36

He quickly recognized her as the woman from the funeral procession. She looked much different now, out of her mourning attire. Apart from her holey, painted-on jeans and tangled blonde hair that hadn't been washed in a week, she was fetching.

"You're defacing private property," the woman declared.

"The thing is, it's not finished," Sam explained. "The gates need detail. It's roughshod, see? I was rushed." Sam went back to work, chiseling away.

"What do you mean, rushed?"

"I did all the work on this stone. I work for Dan's, the grave marker place across the street." Sam pointed toward Dan's even though the building couldn't be seen from where they stood inside the cemetery. Cathy looked over her shoulder toward the cemetery entrance, confused. Sam continued, "I'm just trying to make it look better, that's all."

The woman studied Sam, still skeptical but starting to come around. After all, who would make something like that up? The woman turned her head and examined the stone. It did look better. "What are you doing to it?" she asked.

"Adding detail, mainly. Cleaning up some lines. Dan doesn't really care how they look, as long as they're clean and legible. But I don't put my name on something if I don't believe it's the best it can be."

"Your name's not on it," the woman quipped.

37

"Well, it is and it isn't," Sam retorted. He gazed out as the sun sunk low enough to meet the cemetery tree line, blanketing the field with the shadows of nightfall. Sam struggled to find one knee and stuck his chisel in his back pocket.

"Sun's gone. I'm going to have to come back tomorrow to finish—I mean, if that's okay with you," Sam said, standing up to his full height.

The woman glared at all six-plus feet of him. "I mean, yes, I don't see why not," the woman reckoned. "I'm sorry I raised my voice earlier."

"It's okay, I get yelled at all day," Sam joked as he gently wiped the dust from the stone, polishing it with a rag until it shined again. He turned back toward her. "Are you related?"

"He was my son."

Sam wiped the caked grass from his work shirt. "I'm so sorry," he said. He meant it.

The woman stood silently and folded her arms. It wasn't cold and it wasn't going to be, but in that moment, it might as well have been January. Sam gathered the rest of his tools from the grassy knoll. He felt the woman's gaze on him and he wasn't sure exactly what she wanted him to say. He spied the cemetery gates in the distance.

"They lock those gates at sunset," Sam said. "Just so you know." He moved toward her, their eyes briefly meeting. She watched him as he passed by, and then glanced over toward the cemetery entrance.

"You work in that house with all the tombstones?" she asked.

"That's the one," Sam said with a half smile.

She nodded. "Goodnight."

"Night," he responded, then proceeded to stride the length of the cemetery back to the gates as dusk gave way to twilight. He finally reached the gates and turned back around to see a pair of headlights illuminating the cemetery. It was an eerie and beautiful sight. Sam was halfway down the hill and lost in thought when the low beams suddenly lit him from behind, casting an angelic glow around his tall, Christ-like frame and illuminating the dark, empty neighborhood road in front of him. A car engine pulled close, slowed down then motored parallel with him. He suddenly felt nervous and hyper aware. He looked anxiously toward the car, and was relieved to find it was a Chevy Monte Carlo, driven by the woman from the cemetery—by Ollie Triumph's mother—instead of some Florida meth head with eyes on his wallet.

"You don't have a car?" she asked.

"I'm just walking."

"Where you walking to?" The engine idled. So did Sam. "Up the road a bit," he said.

"You want a ride?"

"That's okay. It's real nice of you though."

"Why don't you just let me give you a ride?"

Sam stared out into the darkness, unsure of what awaited him, both on foot or in the Monte Carlo that rolled next to him at two miles per hour. One thing was for certain, his legs were fucking toast. Sam peered back at the cemetery, then at the woman.

"It seems like a nice night for a walk," he insisted, his mind made up.

#

Three minutes later street lights were sending intermittent streaks of white onto the dashboard of the Monte Carlo as it zoomed through Escapade at twenty-three miles per hour. Sam sat in the passenger seat, his long legs barely fitting in the floor board in front him, his knees bent awkwardly and pressed against the glove compartment.

"The seat goes back," the woman said. "Just use the…the thing." She meant the lever at the bottom of the seat, but as good as Sam was with his hands, he couldn't find that lever if his life depended on it. Sensing his frustration, the woman thrust her arm between his legs and found the damn thing, yanked it back and finally allowed the blood in Sam's lower torso to move freely again.

"Thanks," he said. He studied her in that ridiculous Jimmy Buffett t-shirt and quickly determined that there was no bra underneath it. She caught him in mid-ogle and glared back. He turned away instantly, but he knew he was busted.

"You a big Jimmy Buffett fan?" she asked, blowing through a yellow light that had just turned red.

"Yeah, he's okay," Sam answered.

"You either love Jimmy Buffett or you hate him, there's no in between. I believe that with all of my heart."

"I'm pretty sure I fall somewhere in the middle," Sam countered.

"Nope. There's no middle ground. That's bullshit."

"Okay, let me think about it then." This answer appeased the woman to a certain degree. Sam glanced in the backseat and noticed a guitar case partially covered by scattered clothing items.

"Do you play?" he asked.

She rolled the driver's side window down and tapped cigarette ash on the window's edge. "I do," she said. Sam nodded, impressed.

"I have a guitar but I don't know how to play it," he admitted. "My grandfather left it to me."

"You should learn how to play it," she insisted, continuing her drive into a neighborhood filled with opulent, oversized houses.

"Where am I driving you, by the way?" she asked. "I'm not even really sure where I am." Sam gazed through the passenger window at a section of Escapade he had never seen before. The nice part of town. Where the rich people lived.

"Any one of these will do," Sam joked.

"How about the one with the dolphin fountain out front?" the woman quipped.

"How about the Super 8 on Langston?"

"You live in a fuckin' motel?"

"For the moment. It's a long story … actually, it's not. Did you hear about the sinkhole over on Sunswept Drive?"

"Yeah, yeah," she replied, the cigarette dangling between her full lips. "Big fucking thing, I heard."

"That was across the street from my house," Sam asserted. "I had to move out for thirty days. They're running some environmental tests or something."

"No shit," she laughed. "Ain't that some luck?"

"Yeah, pretty bad luck," Sam said, not laughing nearly as much. Ten minutes later, the Monte Carlo pulled up outside of the Super 8 Motel. Sam climbed out and shut the passenger door, then turned around and glanced back into the car. "Thank you, again. You saved me a long walk."

The woman smiled. Sam gently tapped the hood of the Monte Carlo and set out toward his motel room.

"Hey!" the woman called out. Sam stopped and turned around in the parking lot.

"It was real nice of you to do what you did today," she said. "You didn't have to do that."

"I'll finish it tomorrow," he declared, "I promise." He spun to leave and then turned back one last time "I just realized I never got your name."

The woman grinned, lighting another cigarette as the Monte Carlo idled. "It's Cathy," she said.

"Cathy... I'm Sam," and on that note, Sam climbed the stairs and stuck his key into the lock of Room 212. He looked back over his shoulder as the Monte Carlo smoked out of the parking lot and disappeared into the night. As the exhaust funneled out into the atmosphere, Sam felt something awaken inside of him. Something once lost and now found, like a face he hadn't seen in so long that its contours were no longer recognizable. It felt foreign, this sudden longing. It made his heart beat in a way that he could not control, like cocaine-laced sugar cookies. He was, in a word, smitten.

Sam also recognized that all of these feelings could exist merely because he hadn't eaten all day.

#

Sam paced down the rear motel sidewalk past a trash-filled pool that had would forever remain "temporarily under repair." His destination was a pair of vending machines perched along a brick wall in the distance. Sam found slim pickings: a few bags of expired chips, a year-old pack of Big Red Gum, Tropical Fruit Skittles. The shit no one wants. Sam stuck three quarters into the slot and settled on a fifty-five cent bag of expired FunYuns, watching them retract from their silvery coil and drop to the bottom. Dinner, at last.

CHAPTER SIX

After his first night in the motel and the ensuing late-for-work fiasco, Sam made sure to keep the blackout curtains open enough to allow the sun to do its job in the morning. It was either that, or set the alarm on his Timex, but he never had figured out how to do that.

It wasn't the sun that woke Sam in the morning, but the whoosh of a piece of paper being slid under his door around six-thirty, followed by the obnoxious clomping of Doc Marten boots plodding down a concrete stairwell.

Sam rolled out of bed and grabbed the paper off the carpet. It took a minute for his eyes to adjust, but he soon realized it was a bill summary for his motel stay. Sam coughed until his lungs nearly came up as he searched the dingy room for his work shirt.

45

Five minutes later, Sam stood outside the bulletproof motel window and stared at the ogre inside who clearly didn't sleep or shave and who possibly lived inside the booth. The ogre looked up as Sam arrived but didn't move a muscle apart from taking sips of an unknown liquid from a mug that said "I suffer from CRS disease … Can't Remember Shit."

Sam peered down at the bill summary in his hand and then leaned toward the window. "Yeah, I paid for two nights. I need to pay for two more."

The ogre stared a hole through Sam and let loose a mighty black coffee belch. "You knew you were staying four nights and you only paid for two?"

"Yeah. The thing is... I don't know how long I'm staying." Sam slipped three twenties under the metal payment slot beneath the acrylic window.

"It's seventy-two dollars," the ogre grumbled.

"What?"

"Sev-en-ty-fuck-ing-two-dollars," the ogre grunted, pointing up at a crumbling plastic sign behind him with a list of prices. Friday and Saturday were indeed listed as $36 a night, tax "incuded." Sam stared at the sign a little too long for the ogre's taste. "Hablo ingles, senorita?" he prodded.

Pissed, exhausted and hungry, Sam pulled his remaining cash from his shirt pocket and slid three fives through the win-

46

dow with disgust. He stared at the ogre and awaited his change, finally pressing. "I'm supposed to get three dollars back."

"I don't have any ones," the ogre said.

"Of course you don't," Sam snapped before shaking his head and storming away. The ogre mumbled something incoherent, sipped his coffee and turned the microphone off, stuffing Sam's money into his shirt pocket.

#

Sam dragged in to work and discovered a whopping eight tombstones on the day's schedule. This happened from time to time. It was Florida after all, where people came to die. Sam knew he would have no choice but to use the sand blaster on every single one of them because Dan wouldn't pay overtime. Sam threw his morning glare at Maurice, who hadn't even lit his first cigar of the day, let alone fired up the diamond cutter. All Sam could do was stand and wait for the first blank canvas to begin his motherfucker of a day.

Despite the mountainous work load—and the late start thanks to Maurice—Sam made up for lost time, finishing four markers by lunch. Sam decided to work through his one-hour break, to make it to the cemetery to finish Ollie's grave before nightfall. By three o'clock, the sandblaster was shitting the bed and Sam was forced to troubleshoot, so when quitting time rolled around Sam still had one stone to go. Dan came out at five o'clock and paid him a full day's wages, spying the unfinished marker with another two hours left of work on it. "You gonna finish that last one before you go?" Dan inquired. It was a question, but it might as well have been a command, and it meant Sam would work overtime without pay.

"I'll finish it," Sam said, barely able to hold in his contempt. Dan left without another word and Sam watched him drive away in his stupid goddamn BMW. Sam looked down at the sand blaster in his right hand and wondered what it would do to the back of Dan's skull.

#

Cathy pulled into the cemetery and steered the Monte Carlo down the gravel path that led to her son's grave. She came to a stop in a grass driveway near the grave but didn't shut off the engine, at least not at first. She peered out the windshield, expecting to see Sam there finishing the stone like he had promised. But no one was there. She glared at Ollie's stone, sitting alone and unfinished. Cathy's hopes – whatever they were – dissipated in that moment. She inhaled deeply, killed the car's engine and rolled both of her windows up. The muffled sounds of distant cicadas amplified as the inside of the car quickly became a stifling, airless vacuum.

With beads of sweat dotting her forehead, Cathy loomed at her son's tombstone and felt sudden shame. Shame for driving to this place under false pretenses. Shame for thinking about a tall stranger before her son. Shame for concocting a fantasy in which she connected with someone – finally – in a way that was more than just physical. Shame for thinking she deserved anything other than all the misery the universe could deliver.

Cathy held her breath for as long as she could – forty-five full seconds. In a desperate huff, she finally exhaled, as the air liberated from her lungs, escaped through her mouth and nose and filled the baking car. Her fingers searched for and found the manual crank that allowed her to roll the driver's side window down. As welcome oxygen poured in, Cathy sucked in the fresh cemetery air.

Thirty minutes later, Cathy sat down Indian-style in front of her son's tombstone and closed her eyes, hearing nothing but those cicadas reaching their fever pitch as the sun sunk below the horizon line.

#

Sam didn't leave work until almost nine. He was so drained that he hadn't thought about Ollie's tombstone since he skipped lunch. All he could focus on now was the hunger growing in his stomach and his determination to eat anything other than vending machine fare. He had no desire to head straight to the motel, so he allowed his overworked legs to wander. Through muscle memory, or some unknown motivating force, those tired legs carried him the three miles back to his old neighborhood. It was eleven when Sam found himself at the end of Sunswept Drive. It had been less than a week since the sinkhole had sent him packing, but he suddenly felt nostalgic for the old bungalow.

Sam could see the barricades in the distance, but the landscape was different now, permanently altered. In a few more steps and it became clear. Sylvia's house was gone. Not just torn down, but completely gone. It was as if the house—or Sylvia—had never existed. Sam wriggled past the barricades and approached the dark, fathomless sinkhole. There were no crews on the scene, and no police presence, just a giant fucking void in the ground underneath a night sky filled with blinking stars. Sam approached the edge of the hole, closer than he had ever dared go. He moved slowly, with caution. He leaned forward, over the edge, and stared down into the earth and searched for answers, but there were no revelations at the bottom of the pit. There wasn't even a bottom. Sam stepped back three feet and saw his own house across the street, a sight for sore eyes.

Sam paced across the street and peered through the windows of his house. The power had been disconnected, but he could vaguely see his furniture and belongings. He wandered around to the back yard to investigate. The grass was a little bit long for his taste, but the house seemed secure. There were no broken windows. No doors had been kicked in. His house was doing fine without him. His hunger reaching a breaking point, Sam left en route to the nearest Jack in the Box. He ordered three Jumbo Jacks, ate them quickly, and then made the two-mile hike to his motel room, where he fell asleep within minutes.

CHAPTER SEVEN

Sam had two vivid dreams during the course of the night but when he woke up he couldn't remember either one of them. He laid in bed as his eyes adjusted, staring at the popcorn ceiling, overrun with spider webs, searching their strands for clues that might unlock his sleep reverie. Sam had hoped to wake up recharged and purposeful this morning, but last night's burgers weren't sitting too well. Strangely, he still felt hungry.

Sam hustled downtown and ate a quick bite at Jones Diner – biscuits and gravy with three cups of coffee – before pacing across the street to the post office. Per his usual routine, Sam stuck four twenty dollar bills in a Priority Mail envelope, scribbled an address on the front and then sent the letter on its way. Sam shuffled over to his P.O. Box, opened it, and found it empty. This was not acceptable. He stared a hole through the box as if to manifest a letter out of thin air, but the magic wasn't with him today.

"Goddammit, Gary," Sam said to no one. Frustrated, Sam locked the P.O. Box and bolted from the post office, holding the door open for an elderly man as he exited. Sam scaled a small half-flight of concrete steps and spied the payphone across the street outside the diner. He was on a new mission now. Sam criss-cut across traffic back to Jones Diner only to find the payphone was missing. All that remained was the outer metal shell with the words "Southeast Telecom" printed on one side.

Sam slammed his fist against the empty shell, then scanned the bustling downtown street where everyone except him seemed to have a cell phone. Sam hadn't owned one since moving to Florida. It saved him money and he didn't have anyone he wanted to talk to anyway. Until now. Now he had questions, damn it, and he wanted answers. But he would have to wait.

#

Sam knocked out two tombstones on autopilot before lunch. He always worked faster and more efficiently when he had something on his mind, and that was definitely the case today. Around noon, Dan left for one of his classic two-hour lunch breaks. Sam watched him waddle out to his BMW, plop down in the driver's seat, and back out of the gravel drive en

53

route to wherever the hell he went. Sam took the opportunity to sneak into Dan's office. Once inside, he pulled a folded piece of paper from his wallet, picked up the phone, and dialed. As the phone on the other end rang endlessly, Sam's eyes patrolled Dan's office, mostly out of boredom. He raised an eyebrow when he spotted a small framed photo of twin eight-year-old boys and Dan, all clad in matching police officer costumes. Sam had no idea Dan had any children, let alone twins. Maybe they weren't his children. Maybe they were his nephews. He had no idea if Dan had any siblings, or any friends.

The phone on the other end never stopped ringing. Frustrated, Sam hung up and slouched down in Dan's chair. From this angle he could see into the back yard where he spotted Maurice sleeping on top of a giant slab of black granite. Sam just shook his head at the sight. That son of a bitch sure loved to take naps on his lunch break, Sam thought. But the longer he stared, the more uncomfortable he became. Surely, Maurice's chest was rising. It was rising, right? Sam's eyes narrowed.

A moment later, Sam careened slowly through the backyard toward Maurice, who still hadn't moved a muscle. Sam moved closer, stopping about ten feet away from him. "Maurice?" Sam cocked his head and tried to spot any sign of movement. Nothing. He took two more steps forward.

"Hey, Maurice. Lunch is over. Can you hear me?"

Maurice did not respond. His body remained flat and stiff on top of the granite. Sam took another couple of steps, close enough to touch him now.

"Maurice?"

Sam inched even closer, their faces now centimeters apart. He searched desperately for signs of air escaping from Maurice's nose or mouth. He simply couldn't tell. Sam closed his eyes and pressed his ear against Maurice's nose, listening for life as birds chirped loudly overhead. Just as the birds calmed their cries, Sam felt a sudden, piercing pain in his right ear followed by a deafening, high-pitched ringing. He had just been head butted by a terrified Maurice, who had bolted upright on the slab upon awakening to find a man's face pressed against his.

"Motherfucker, what are you doing?" Maurice yelled, grabbing his swollen forehead. Sam peeled himself up from the ground, his right palm pinned to his right ear.

"Fuck, man. I'm sorry. I thought you were dead."

"You thought I was dead?"

"It didn't look like you were breathing."

"I was fuckin' sleeping!"

"I'm sorry. Christ."

Sam lowered his hand from his ear and noticed it was stained with small streaks of blood. "Jesus, you really fucked up my ear, man."

"Don't you bring Jesus into this, you stupid motherfucker."

Sam peered over the fence to see Dan clambering out of his BMW. Fucking great. He backed away from Maurice.

Sam limped into the bathroom, where he rummaged through cabinets until he found cotton balls. He stuck two of them into his ear to soak up the blood slowly draining from his ear. He haphazardly tore off two pieces of blue painter's tape, usually reserved for masking his engravings, and stuck them across his ear to keep the cotton balls in place. With this current look, he resembled someone who had been attacked by a Smurf with claws. He returned to his work station to find Maurice glaring at him from the other side of the yard.

"The hell happened to you?" Dan called out from the patio.

Sam spun around. "I fell on a... I fell."

"If you're gonna kill yourself by cracking your head on a stone, at least engrave the thing first so we don't have to," Dan said with a smirk. He shook his head and went back inside. Sam looked back over at Maurice just in time to see him turn on the diamond saw. The blade screamed through the stone, SCCCRRRCCCHHH!!! Sam clutched his right ear. The vibrations sent shockwaves deep inside his ear drum, which may or may not have been punctured by a vicious head butt from an eighty-year-old black man with sleep apnea. The throbbing was brutal, but Sam somehow made it through the rest of his day.

As Dan doled out the day's pay, he stared at the pink-tinted cotton balls awkwardly taped to Sam's face. "I took out four dollars for the tape," Dan said, kidding but not kidding. Sam pretended he didn't hear him, stuck the cash in his upper left shirt pocket and set out on foot into the Florida evening.

#

On the walk back to his motel, Sam stopped in a KFC bathroom to inspect the damage to his ear. He peeled off the painter's tape slowly and intently, grimacing as the adhesive pulled against his sideburns. The wad of blood-soaked cotton spilled out of his ear and landed on the dirty bathroom floor below. "Goddammit," Sam muttered, the pain so intense he could feel his pulse thumping inside his ear. He turned his head to the right to get a better view of the situation. The cotton balls had soaked up most of the blood but had left a thick, dried pool of it on the inside of his ear. Sam tenderly guided his fingers inside the canal, wincing as they made contact. Fucking Maurice had really done a number on him.

"How'd you hurt your ear?" a voice called out from behind. Between the echo of the ceramic-tiled bathroom and the vacuum effect caused by a blown ear drum, it sounded as if the voice of God had spoken inside the lone stall of a Kentucky Fried Chicken men's room. Sam turned around expecting a deity, but instead he saw the back of a three-hundred-pound, middle-aged

57

heart attack waiting to happen wearing an embroidered American flag dress shirt tucked into jean shorts. Sam acknowledged the man with a head nod but didn't answer him. He exited the bathroom as quickly as he could and continued his journey back to the motel.

#

As night arrived, Sam hoped the slight dip in temperature might soothe the pulsing pain in his ear, but every footstep sent sharp needles deep into his head. Sam limped along, trying not to focus on his discomfort. His hearing had shifted as well. What was previously a muffled vacuum had now become a muffled vacuum accompanied by a sharp, insufferable ringing, a non-stop modem dialing inside of him. Sam stopped a half mile from the motel, unable to take it anymore. "Fuck this," he gasped, collapsing on a bus bench as headlights from passing cars strobed in and out of his peripheral vision.

Sam was sitting as still as possible with his eyes clenched tight. "Does this bus go downtown?" a voice asked.

He opened his eyes to see the man from the KFC bathroom, completely oblivious to Sam's discomfort. Sam closed his eyes again, and did not reply. A few minutes later, a bus pulled up and Sam felt the weight on the bench shift. He opened his eyes to see the man in the embroidered American flag shirt climb on a bus headed nowhere near downtown. The man chose a window seat three rows from the front. He eyed Sam and waved as the bus zoomed away. It was a gesture that was not reciprocated. Sam immediately felt like an asshole.

Sam contemplated his next move. The ringing wasn't going away and neither was the pain. Before he could make a decision, a woman's voice called out.

"Hey!"

With only one good ear, Sam couldn't tell which direction the voice was coming from. He stretched around to the left, but saw no one.

"Hey! Sam!" the voice called out again. Sam twisted around to the right and saw Cathy standing next to her car, with the driver's side door open, in a slimy strip mall parking lot behind the bus stop.

"Oh … hey," Sam said.

"You just missed the bus," Cathy mused.

"No. There's another one," Sam said. He clutched his right ear as the echo of his own voice sent ripples of pain through every cell in his body.

Cathy closed her car door and took a few steps toward Sam. "You okay?" she asked

"I'm fine," Sam insisted. "I just hurt my ear."

Cathy approached Sam to get a closer look. "Let me see."

"It's fine, I'm... "

Cathy attempted to pry Sam's hand away from his ear but his grip held tight. She responded with a stronger one and Sam acquiesced, letting loose of his ear. Cathy moved closer to get a look inside his ear. Sam felt her warm breath on his neck and for a split second the pain went away. It didn't stay gone long. Cathy angled his head toward the street light and proclaimed, "Damn, this doesn't look good."

"It's my ear drum," Sam said, "I'm pretty sure it burst."

"How do you know?"

"Because I know."

"You need to see a doctor," she said. "Come with me."

"I don't have money for a doctor."

"There's a free clinic a mile from here."

Cathy grabbed his arm and pulled him up from the bench. "Come on, don't be a baby."

#

Sam lay fully reclined in the passenger seat with his right ear pressed against the headrest as Cathy steered the Monte Carlo toward parts unknown. From his vantage point, Sam could see nothing out the window except passing street lamps which intermittently illuminated his face with streaks of harsh, unwanted flashes. For all he knew, Cathy could be taking him hostage, but he didn't care at this point. The pain was that intense. Cathy maneuvered into South Escapade, the poorest part of town, where local businesses displayed more signs in Spanish than in English.

"Where are you taking me?" Sam asked as the car slowed to a crawl.

Cathy pulled into a strip mall and parked in front of a small hole in the wall with a lighted sign that read "Clinico Medico, 24 Ahoras." Cathy helped Sam out of the car and guided him toward a clinic that was sandwiched between a laundromat and a convenience store. "I got the morning after pill here once," Cathy boasted.

"At the laundromat?" Sam replied.

#

An Hispanic doctor in a white coat embroidered with the name "Mendoza" spent about forty-five seconds gazing into Sam's ear canal with an otoscope. Sam jerked when the tip of the instrument reached his inner canal. "Hold still, please," Dr. Mendoza demanded. Sam was never a good patient.

Cathy sat in a metal folding chair in the corner of the tiny exam room next to a poster showing the stages of pregnancy. Dr. Mendoza finally retreated from Sam's ear and slipped a sterile cap off the end of the otsocope, tossing it into a nearby trash can. "You bust your ear drum," he said. "How you bust your ear drum?" Sam opened his eyes and glared at Cathy. He didn't say it out loud, but his eyes said, *I told you so*.

61

"I had an accident at work," Sam explained. Dr. Mendoza removed the latex gloves from his hands.

"Nothing we can really do but wait you heal. You rest. Sleep on other ear. We give you some drops." Sam frowned and nodded. Live with the pain until the pain was gone. That was a process he understood well.

Sam and Cathy spilled back into the parking lot to find the Monte Carlo still in one piece, luckily. Sam was still in a lot of discomfort but having Cathy there helped take the edge off. When they reached the car, Sam twisted the top off of a small bottle of ear drops, tilted his head to the side and squeezed a few into his ear. He grimaced as the thick antibiotic seeped through his canal.

"I hate this shit," Sam groaned.

"Where are we going now?" Cathy asked. Sam rotated the lid back on the ear drop bottle. "I think I just need to lie down."

Cathy unlocked the driver's side door, climbed in, then reached across the seat to unlock the passenger door from the inside. The Monte Carlo was a unique beast. She got you where you were going but never made it easy on you. Sam watched the lock slide up on the passenger door and caught Cathy's soft glance through the window. It was a spellbinding moment, seeing her through dirt and fingerprint-speckled glass, her features illuminated by the strip mall security light. Sam had always enjoyed looking at people through windows, it was as if the small buffer of glass opened up a temporary portal into someone's psyche. He had memories of his mother picking him up from elementary school, her shoulder-length brown hair bouncing against her frame as she smiled and waved at him from the blue Ford Escort that she drove until the day she drove it away for good.

Sam slipped into Cathy's car and sunk into the vinyl seat.

"I don't live far from here," Cathy said. "Why don't you sleep at my place tonight? I've got some vicodin at the house."

Through the pounding inside of his head, Sam thought about the absolute shit night of no sleep he was doomed to have if he went back to the motel. He caught Cathy in his peripheral. He had no idea why this woman was taking such a sudden interest in him, apart from their chance meeting at the cemetery and his efforts to beautify her dead son's tombstone, but he was too tired to fight the idea.

"Yeah, okay."

Cathy smiled and cranked the engine. "I'm gonna drive through Carl's Jr.'s first if that's okay." Sam agreed, his stomach suddenly growling. Sam found the lever at the front of his seat quickly this time around, and promptly yanking it until his seat reached its fully reclined position. As the Monte Carlo bid farewell to the parking lot, lights danced and spun across the windshield like a makeshift planetarium display. Sam closed his eyes as the road rumbled underneath him.

#

Sam awoke alone to the undeniable smell of fast food. He was still in the car, which was parked in an unknown driveway. As he lifted his seat to its upright position, Sam noticed the driver's-side door was open, and the dome light was on. An incessant "ding, ding, ding" alerted him that the keys were still in the ignition. Cathy came back into view outside the car. "Had to get the mail," she said, reaching into the car and pulling out the keys. "Home sweet home," she declared.

The neighborhood landscape looked totally foreign to Sam. He spied the neighbor's house across the street and saw a boat, then two more crafts sandwiched between other houses. He was definitely still in Escapade.

Cathy led Sam into a bungalow not unlike the one he called home, but even more run down. "It's just a rental," she said. "I've been looking for something else for awhile."

Cathy stuck her key in the lock, jiggled it for an eternity, then finally won the battle. Sam followed her inside, unsure of what awaited him, but too exhausted to care. A small foyer led to a sunken living room filled with mismatched furniture and recessed lighting straight out of the eighties. In the corner, a small TV sat on top of a larger one. Neither set seemed to be in working condition. A red brick fireplace filled the far wall, its mantle lined with family photos.

"We can eat in here or in the kitchen. I usually eat in the kitchen," she said.

"Kitchen's good," Sam replied.

Sam and Cathy sat at a small wooden table in an impossibly tiny kitchen eating out of their respective grease bags. Sam devoured his burger quickly, then set out to speed-eat his fries. A slack-jawed Cathy watched him like a spectator at an eating competition. "Better check the bag and make sure you didn't leave any behind," she joked.

"Sorry, I was hungry," Sam said before actually taking Cathy's advice and checking the bag where he did indeed find, and then devour, two more fries. Sam glanced around a kitchen and discovered a sink full of dishes and liquor bottles. Food bags and miscellaneous trash lay scattered across the counter. To say the place was a mess was putting it nicely. Sam studied Cathy as she ate. This was a woman who clearly lived alone and had little drive or desire to keep things clean. He then remembered that this was also a woman who had just lost her son and that he didn't know the circumstances surrounding that tragedy. His eyes glazed over, and he didn't even notice her staring a hole through him.

"What are you thinking about?" Cathy asked. Sam's eyes drifted back to the sink.

"I was thinking I'd like to do that sink full of dishes. It's the least I can do, after what you did tonight."

"Those dishes aren't goin' anywhere," Cathy insisted. She peeled away from the cramped table and veered toward the kitchen cabinets. Sam watched her. She looked back briefly, feeling his glances. Her light-washed Lee jeans were impossibly tight, and when she reached high in the cupboard to pull out two shot glasses, her blouse opened up just enough to reveal a black bra underneath. Her breasts weren't anything to write home about, but there they were.

Cathy wandered to a dented refrigerator plastered with a child's manic crayon drawings. Cathy reached deep into the freezer and emerged with a frosted bottle of cheap tequila. She returned to the table and filled two shot glasses, one slightly less than the other. She set the full one in front of Sam. "Your ear will thank you, trust me."

Sam smiled and picked up his shot. He glanced at Cathy's t-shirt. "To Jimmy Buffett, wherever he is."

#

Sam found himself alone in a small shower being pelted with water that he was certain contained ice - it was that fucking cold. He desperately twisted the knob marked "H" but it had

66

little effect on the temperature of the water. The good news and bad news in this situation were exactly the same: Sam was sobering up. He finished the shower as quickly as he could, then stepped out and toweled off his shivering torso. He glanced down at the cold black and white tile where he had placed his clothes. They were gone.

Sam turned an antique glass doorknob and opened the creaky bathroom door. He could hear music, and saw Cathy sitting on her bed with a well-worn guitar. It was covered in bumps, bruises, scratches and cracks, but sound still managed to come out of it. It represented Cathy well in that regard. Cathy looked up when he stuck his head out of the bathroom. She strummed the same chord over and over, trying to find a melody in her head, staring at Sam the whole time without ever really seeing him. She focused on her fingers as they stretched across the fret board.

Sam stepped into the bedroom with a towel wrapped around his waist. Cathy continued to pluck at the strings. "Sorry about the cold water," she said. "Water heater went out and the damn landlord is too cheap to replace it."

"Oh. It's okay," Sam muttered through still-chattering teeth as he glanced around the room in search of his garments. "Did you take my clothes?"

Cathy nodded. "I washed them. I hope that was okay."

"Oh. Sure. Thank you."

He stood, uncertain of his next move.

"They'll be done in about ten minutes," she reassured him, her playing suddenly stopped. Sam could feel her eyes on him. Feeling somewhat exposed, he sat down on the edge of the bed as Cathy resumed her soft strumming behind him.

"That's really pretty," he said, flashing a glance back at her. "I wish I could hear it with both ears. Did you write that?"

"I did," Cathy said with a sheepish smile. Suddenly self-conscious, Cathy slid the guitar down beside the bed, leaning it against the night stand.

"I made you a bed in the other room," she said. "You can go on in. I'll set your clothes outside the door in a few minutes."

Sam stood up. "Thank you again," he said, tequila and Vicodin swimming together in his system. "You really didn't have to."

Cathy shook her head. "I don't mind good company."

Sam crept out of her bedroom into a small, dark hallway that led toward three closed doors. The door at the end of the hall – probably a linen closest – featured a wood grain pattern that appeared to take the shape of a tall, thin apparition with bulbous arms and legs stretched out to the edges. The pattern startled Sam and he almost feared moving past it before his bravery won out. His eyes clenched, Sam ducked through the

68

only door with light spilling out from around its edges. He would be totally unprepared for what waited inside.

Sam stood in a child's bedroom. Ollie's room. A room that had clearly remained unchanged since its inhabitant had vanished. A toddler-sized bed still had its covers pulled back—this was the bed that Cathy had prepared for him. There was a small dresser with a baseball glove painted on the side parked against the wall, a rogue sock stuck out of the top drawer. Attached to the ceiling was a Styrofoam model of the solar system stretching from one side of the room to the other. Underneath, a wildly off-balance ceiling fan whistled and spun like a doomed helicopter, blades rattling and motor moaning. Toys were scattered around the carpet. It was as if Ollie would be coming back at any moment to claim his domain.

Bewildered, Sam sat down on the bed and allowed the unwanted ringing in his right ear drown out his thoughts. For the first time, Sam appreciated the distraction.

Footsteps came and went outside the bedroom door. Sam got up, peeked out and found his clothing, clean and folded. He quietly slipped on his underwear and a white t-shirt, turned out the light that kindled from a single bulb above, then stuffed his lengthy frame under linens with a space ship design. His calves, ankles and feet extended well beyond the mattress. Nothing about it felt right, physically or emotionally. Sam slid out of the bed and found his sleeping bag in the dark. He quietly unzipped it and slinked inside. A lone lamppost at the edge of the driveway funneled a streak of light through a broken mini-blind, and Sam's eyes soon adjusted to the darkness. His gazed up at the ceiling where a luminous display began to form in the blackness. Dozens of glow-in-the-dark stars twinkled across the bedroom ceiling. Sam counted them like boats but soon lost track of their total. They reminded him of nights spent in the cemetery, laying on the cool grass and gawking at the endless macrocosm spread out above him. Sam fell asleep with Cathy's song stuck in his head, and he dreamt that he was piloting an airplane with no passengers through a cloudless sky to an unknown destination. The dream made him feel new and amazing, but when he awoke he had no recollection of it.

CHAPTER EIGHT

By the time Sam crawled out of his sleeping bag the next morning, he was certain it must be afternoon. Sam could've blamed the tequila for the pounding and throbbing in his head, but he knew it was his ear. He reached into his work shirt on the floor and retrieved his ear drops. He squeezed three into his ear and his eyes went watery. He glanced up at the ceiling as the liquid oozed slowly toward his ear drum, and he was surprised to find the plaster completely devoid of glow-in-the-dark stars. Sam blinked the tears out of his eyes and looked again, but ceiling was definitely bare. Sam wanted to chalk this odd occurrence up to fatigue, but he began to wonder exactly what he had seen the night before, and if he really did hear that beautiful song come out of that heartbroken woman.

71

Sam found Cathy sitting on the living room floor with her knees up to her chin watching a Spanish soap opera on the smaller TV which sat atop the larger one. No sound emerged from the tiny TV's speaker – it was either muted or broken.

"Morning," he yawned, massaging his ear. "It is still morning, isn't it?"

Cathy looked up. "Think so. How's the ear?"

"I'll survive."

"Did you sleep okay?"

"I did," Sam assured her, glancing around the cluttered house. Junk was crammed in every corner. He studied the TV. "What are you watching?"

"I don't know, but these people are very animated," Cathy said. Her eyes peeled away from the TV long enough to look up at Sam. "There's some old bagels in the fridge. Don't have any cream cheese though."

"Thanks, but I should probably get back to the motel."

"I'll take you there on my way to work," she said.

#

Sam trailed Cathy out of the house toward her car. "Don't get in just yet," she muttered, popping the rusted hood on the Monte Carlo and forcefully yanking it open.

"Car trouble?" Sam asked.

Cathy picked up a gallon of pre-mixed coolant from the ankle-high grass next to the driveway. She twisted off a cap on the engine and haphazardly poured the blue liquid into its receptacle. Half of it ended up spilling on the battery.

"I could help you with that," Sam said. Before it was even a possibility, Cathy had slammed the hood back down and tossed the coolant jug back in the grass.

"Preventative maintenance," she said.

"Never hurts," Sam said, standing outside the passenger window.

"You can get in now," Cathy instructed.

The white-hot morning sun beamed through the windshield as Sam and Cathy tooled through Escapade at twenty-five miles per hour. They cruised past strip malls and neighborhoods, boats and dollar stores, bus stops and churches, fathers hugging their daughters outside of police stations. Somewhere along the way, Sam glanced over at Cathy and watched the wind from the open driver's window whip her hair around. He enjoyed the chaos and the beauty, and he regretted leaving her house so abruptly. He didn't know this woman from Adam, but he felt connected to her in a way that was impossible to explain.

"That's where I work," Cathy blurted as they drove past the strip mall where Cathy had rescued Sam the night before.

"At the Seven-Eleven?"

73

"No, next door," Cathy said, pointing to a tiny space with blacked out windows and a lighted neon sign above the door that simply read "RJ."

"Oh. What is that?"

"RJ's Games and Stuff."

"Is it like an arcade?"

Cathy grinned. "Sort of … You never heard of it?"

"No."

Cathy stopped at a red light and lit a cigarette. The smoke stung Sam's eyes but he found the whole routine strangely romantic. "It's all eight-liners. Slot machines." She leaned in close to Sam's face for no other reason than to be dramatic. Her voice lowered to a whisper. "It's a fucking gambling hall," she said with a wink.

The light turned green and Cathy hit the gas. Sam mulled it over. "Is that legal?"

Cathy flicked her cigarette ashes out the window. "I mean… yeah, we don't give out cash. That would be illegal. The prizes are gift cards. Wal-Mart, Chili's, shit like that. You should come check it out."

Sam appeared impressed. "Okay," he said, almost excitedly.

Cathy pulled into the Super 8 just as the ogre from the front desk was stuffing a large black trash bag into the dumpster at the end of the parking lot. He glanced at the Monte Carlo as it approached, then resumed stuffing the garbage or the body or whatever the hell it was into the metal trash bin.

"This place looks lovely," Cathy said. "How are the accommodations?" She found an open spot next to a dented Ford Focus with a broken rear windshield and pulled in. Sam and Cathy watched in amazement as the ogre used a metal rake to jam the trash bag farther into the dumpster.

Sam sighed. "It's just for a few more weeks."

"Then you can move back into your house?"

"I hope so. That's the plan."

The ogre, now in a full sweat, struggled to close the overflowing dumpster lid before finally succeeding. He retrieved his rake from the concrete and walked past the parked Monte Carlo, firing a lifeless look at Sam and Cathy as he limped by on his way back to his bulletproof magazine-reading closet.

"How much are you paying to stay at this shit hole?" Cathy inquired.

"Thirty a night. Thirty-seven on weekends."

"What a fuckin' rip off."

"I know," Sam admitted. Cathy studied him as he sat there in his work shirt, deep in thought. He took a long breath and observed the rusted metal staircase that led to his room. "Well, I guess I should get going. Thank you again for-"

"Move in with me," Cathy blurted, her eyes open and full of anticipation. Sam sat silent, more stunned than anything.

"What?" he finally responded.

"There's no point in you wasting your money in this dump for three more weeks. I don't mind the company. You can use the car if you need it."

"I don't drive."

Cathy wrinkled her eyebrows. "You don't drive."

A thousand thoughts raced through Sam's head as he stared up at the filthy, rotting shit box he called his temporary home. He worked out the math in his head, figuring he'd save damn near eight hundred dollars over three weeks—money he could really use.

"What are you thinking about?" Cathy asked.

Sam finally snapped out of his philosophical/mathematical daze. "It's real nice of you," he said. "I just don't want to impose."

"Dude, look at me. You're not imposing at all." Cathy's rough edge quickly softened as she had trouble holding back a sly grin. Sam's body language eased. She was winning him over, but before he could say anything, the door to Room 106 flew open and a domestic argument between a meth head in a tank top and his topless heroin addict girlfriend spilled out onto the sidewalk in front of the Monte Carlo. A screaming match ensued. The woman took a swing at the man, clocking him in the jaw, sending him reeling onto the hood of the dented Ford Focus. Meth-head found his balance, spit out two bloody teeth, and charged back at his girlfriend. The ogre appeared with his metal rake, pointing it at the meth head, who spit blood at the ogre before sprinting out of the parking lot. The ogre turned the rake toward the girlfriend. "Get out of my fucking motel!"

Sam looked at Cathy. "Okay. You talked me into it."

Sam managed to cram all of his belongings - his sleeping bag, his guitar case, and his records - into the back seat of the Monte Carlo. Cathy started the car and fired a look at Sam. "Do you need to check out first?"

As they drove away from the motel, Sam felt a warm feeling in the pit of his stomach that simultaneously excited him and scared him. Cathy pushed the Monte Carlo a little faster than usual, as if she couldn't wait to get Sam as far away from that place as possible. As the midday sun beat down through the windshield, Sam closed his eyes and fantasized that he was being kidnapped. Adrenaline flooded Sam's entire body and he wondered what it would be like to die from cancer on the happiest day of his life.

#

Sam and Cathy had spent most of the afternoon and early evening eating taquitos from 7-Eleven and drinking Boone's

Farm wine mixers on the couch in the living room. High class dining it was not, but the pair was content to be lost in each other's company. The TV had been stuck on the same channel for hours—a static-filled Mexican network that played a variety of game shows that always seemed to feature a dwarf in a cowboy hat and large-breasted women in swimsuits.

Sam hadn't been this drunk in years, and as each laugh grew louder he became distracted by the volume of his voice. He suddenly found himself in that hollow, down in a tunnel sort of drunken state that feels good while you're there but so goddamn awful coming back. Sam didn't care about later, all he knew right now was that his insides were balmy and he was enjoying the company of a woman who liked fast food as much as he did.

"Why don't you play that thing?" Cathy said.

Sam had no idea what Cathy was referring until he followed her eyes to his guitar case sitting by the front door. "I told you. I don't know how."

"Why do you have a guitar if you don't know how to play it?"

"My grandfather left it to me. He played. My brother got seven thousand dollars from him. I got this guitar, and those records."

"Open it up," Cathy requested as she finished off the last of a green apple Boone's. Sam climbed off the couch and stumbled toward the door, nearly losing his footing. Cathy laughed. Sam picked up the case and carried it back to the couch. He sat down with the case in his lap, and ran his hands over the brown tweed that covered the top, back and sides. His fingers found the metal clasps. The top lifted with four metallic clicks.

"Holy shit," Cathy bellowed, her wide eyes peering inside. The acoustic guitar had a beautifully aged, red-gold finish with mahogany sides. The pick guard featured an intricate stencil of a bird sitting on a branch and the fret board was adorned with striking pearloid inlays. The guitar was covered in nicks and scratches and patina, in all the right places. This wasn't a collector's guitar—it had been played and played a lot.

Sam met Cathy's glowing gaze. "Is it a good one?" he asked.

"That's a Gibson Dove," Cathy said, assuming Sam would get the reference. She leaned in close and peeked inside the sound hole. Her dishwater blonde hair brushed against Sam's arm. "Does it have a label inside?" she asked.

"I don't know. Does it?"

Cathy peered inside the sound hole. No label. Didn't matter. Cathy was in love. She had never held such a beautiful guitar.

"This is a late fifties model, I bet. Original finish too. You see all this finish checking?"

"I don't know what that means," Sam admitted.

Cathy ran her fingers along the top of the guitar near the pick guard. "You see these tiny little surface cracks that run all over the top? They're like rings in a tree. They tell you the history of the guitar."

Sam picked up the guitar and stuck his nose in the sound hole. "It smells like my grandfather's house."

"They don't make 'em like this anymore."

"Do you want to play it?"

Cathy nearly fell off the couch. "What do you think?"

Sam handed the guitar to her. She gently wrapped her hand around the contours of the neck and allowed the guitar to sink into her lap. Its curves perfectly conformed to her legs and the cool, aged mahogany felt so good against them. It wasn't every day that she got to see, let alone play, an instrument like this. She moved her left hand into a chord position on the fret board.

Cathy began to pluck the strings independently, picking them with the flat part of her fingers. It was a resplendent, confident sound, and a melody burst out of the guitar as bright as any star had ever burned. Cathy closed her eyes and sang ...

A two lane highway

Headlights are on the horizon line

So far from here, but I know something's comin'

Sam felt the words hit him like a truck. He stared as she continued...

And you say words fail
but I know it's all in the way they sound
when spoken aloud… do you wish I never said it?
And you, you say the worst is over now
the best years of our life are yet to come
but maybe it's meant to be a mystery

Cathy closed her eyes tightly and picked a perfect melody to match the vocal line. Sam had never heard something so beautiful. The instrumental section ended, leading into another verse…

And we, we crashed this thing a hundred times
but the wheels just kept on spinnin' and turnin' around
and maybe that's how it had to be

The soft picking made way for hard strums now as Cathy's eyes filled with tears that she refused to release. Her strums reached a crescendo and then suddenly fell soft as she sang one last verse…

A two lane highway
Headlights are on the horizon line
so far from here, but I know something's coming

Cathy picked the melody one more time then let the last chord ring out as long as the vintage guitar would let it. When it was over, she felt Sam's eyes all over her. She immediately turned red.

"Anyway ..."

"That was so good," Sam marveled. "Did you write that?"

Cathy nodded, noticing that the clock read 7:03.

"Shit! I'm late!" Cathy exclaimed. She handed the guitar back to Sam, jumped up from the couch and heaved her yellow summer dress up and over her head, tossing it to the hardwood floor below. She made a beeline for the hallway, wearing nothing but a bra and panties. In the melee, Sam damn near dropped the guitar. Cathy re-appeared wearing jeans and a black polo shirt with the "RJ's Gameroom" logo stitched into the left breast.

"I'll be back late. There's some stuff in the fridge," Cathy bellowed before flying out of the house in a frenzy. Sam watched from the front porch as the Monte Carlo backed out of the drive and vanished into the night. Sam suddenly noticed a knot in the pit of his stomach that had not been there before. He turned back toward the front door but before he could make it he puked up five taquitos and three bottles of Boone's Farm all over an innocent azalea plant.

Sam spent the next two hours listening to the echoes of his own footsteps as they creaked across the hardwood floors in Cathy's living room, each one booming loudly in Sam's deeply damaged ear. As he sobered, Sam realized that being alone in such a quiet place made him think about his home, about the growing sinkhole and what might become of his house in the days ahead. Sam appreciated Cathy, and was grateful for her hospitality, but he desperately missed his routine. He was a creature of habit, and right now he was about a million miles out of his comfort zone.

Sam's footsteps carried him into Cathy's backyard where a child's tricycle sat upside down amongst knee-high grass and overgrown weeds. A privacy fence surrounded the yard but offered little actual "privacy" as several planks were missing, bent, or littered with holes. In the back corner of the yard, to Sam's amazement, stood a banana tree much like the one he owned, but smaller. He approached the young, unruly sapling which clearly hadn't seen much attention. Its limbs stretched up nine feet at the most. Its fruit grew small and unimpressive, but the thing had spirit. It glared at Sam as if to say "I'm going to be huge someday, motherfucker." Sam believed it. The tree made him think about Ollie, the young boy he never met but whose bedroom he was now sleeping in. What kind of kid had he been? And what had happened to him? He hadn't yet built up the nerve to ask Cathy about it, and he wondered if he ever would.

Sam took one long, last glance at the tree before turning back toward the house. He remembered that the bonsai tree on the back patio of his house hadn't been watered in days, and he made a mental reminder to retrieve it after work tomorrow. As he reached the back door, he felt something wet on his right ear. He swiped it with his hand and checked his fingers to discover a thick mucus-like substance. He held it up to his nose and sniffed it – something awful. He hoped this meant his ear was healing.

#

Cathy's cell phone stared at Sam from its perch on the kitchen counter. He had ignored its beacon for the last couple of hours now, but as the night wore on, he finally gave in to temptation. Sam glanced at the LED display on the gas stove in the kitchen. It read 10:35 p.m. *It's nine-thirty there*, Sam thought before scooping up the phone and dialing ten numbers. The line rang twelve excruciating times before a voice mail kicked in on the other end.

"This is Gary, leave a message." Click. BEEP.

Sam stared at the phone and then hung it up. He dialed again. The line rang twelve more times.

"This is Gary, leave a message." Click. BEEP.

"Hey man, it's me. I've been sending you those envelopes. Are you getting 'em? You're supposed to be sending me updates. I wish you'd answer your phone. Anyway, let me know what's going on. You can call me on this number if you want." Sam disconnected the call and stared at the phone, frustrated.

Sam laid down on the couch in the living room and watched TV for an hour or so. Whether it was the unfamiliar surroundings or the sudden solitude or the churning in his mind that never seemed to cease, Sam's eyes refused to stay closed. He thought about Cathy at work and wondered what she was doing. Then, for some reason, despite the fact that he had to go to work in less than eight hours, Sam decided to walk to the strip mall to check out the game room.

It was a much longer walk than he had expected, but Sam finally reached the strip mall around midnight. The parking lot sat flooded with cars and a few stragglers and ne'er-do-wells loitered outside the 7-Eleven. Sam stared at the blackened windows of the "arcade" with no idea what he might find inside.

Sam entered the dank, poorly-lit entertainment zone and immediately felt claustrophobic. The game room was long and narrow with sides flanked by dozens of eight-liner slot machines from the front all the way to the back. Another two rows crammed the middle, leaving two tiny aisles of walk space. The electronic jingle-jangle of winners and losers created a never-ending loop of dings, bells, exclamations and expletives. The air was choking thick with cigarette smoke and desperation. The sting of smoke from Marlboro Reds made Sam's eyes feel like they were slowly filling with flames. He squinted and blinked to refresh them, on the lookout for Cathy.

"ID," a voice called out from somewhere in the madness. Sam scanned the room and found the "redemption desk," a glass display case with assorted gifts and prizes. The voice belonged to a muscled-up bouncer type with a mustache and the same black polo shirt that Cathy had left the house wearing.

"I'm just looking for someone," Sam said.

"Buy some tokens or get out," the steroid-fueled hulk wheezed. His clenched fists were filled with wads of cash, and a vein the size of the San Andreas fault protruded from his neck. Sam decided this wasn't a battle worth fighting, so he quickly produced his Florida driver's license and bought ten dollars worth of tokens. The lug handed him a plastic bucket filled with gold-colored coins, all emblazoned with the "RJ" logo.

"Good luck," the monster smirked.

Sam wandered until he found an empty slot machine sandwiched between a couple of chain-smoking fatsos. He sat down and pulled a token from his bucket and glanced around for Cathy. He began to wonder if she really worked here. Figuring he was already in Rome, Sam dropped a token into the machine and pulled the handle. Three mechanical wheels whirled and stopped on cherry, lemon, and grapes. Sam was not a winner. He dropped in another token and repeated the process, with the same result. This didn't appear to be his night.

"What are you doing here?"

Sam spun around and found Cathy in her uniform, holding a waitress tray. She looked shocked to see him, but pleasantly surprised. She also appeared stressed.

"Just wanted to see what all the fuss was about," Sam declared. He glanced at her tray, brimming with drinks. "So this is what you do?"

Cathy shook her head and rolled her eyes. "I normally work up front, but one of the waitresses quit, so I had to cover the floor tonight. You want something?"

After his run-in with the azalea, Sam was clearly in no mood to continue his night of drinking. "I think I'm still recovering from earlier," he declared.

"You sure? They're free. We can't sell 'em." She leaned in and whispered, "no liquor license."

Upon hearing this news, Sam decided that a free drink of any kind was probably too good to pass up. "I guess I'll take a beer, then."

"CATHY! WE NEED TOKENS!" an urgent voice yelled from the front. Cathy rolled her eyes again. "I gotta fuckin' do everything here. I'll be back with that beer." She turned to leave but spun back around, leaning close to Sam's good ear. "That machine over there is a winner." Her eyes directed him to a vacant slot machine on the end of his row.

87

Two hours later Sam was up almost three hundred dollars on the hot machine and he'd completely lost track of time. At two a.m. sharp, rows of fluorescent lights suddenly gleamed from the ceiling above, flooding the dark arcade in a wall of harsh, sobering light. In this vivid new world, Sam could see how truly filthy this place was, and he realized it was way past time to cash out. Before Sam made his way up to the front, Cathy snuck by and whispered "Take the crafts gift card, trust me." This request baffled Sam because it meant passing up three hundred dollars worth of Wal-Mart, Applebee's and Chili's re-demptions. Instead, he cashed out with three hundred dollars redeemable at Martha's Craft Emporium in beautiful downtown Escapade. He was certain he would later regret this decision.

Cathy finally clocked out around two-fifteen and found Sam standing outside the 7-Eleven sipping a tall fountain drink and stuffing a hot dog in his mouth.

"Breakfast of champions?" she joked.

"Well, it is morning," Sam replied with a mouth full of hot dog. "I got you one too."

Sam extended a paper sleeve her way containing 99 cents worth of nitrates and three days worth of sodium. Cathy accept-ed it graciously and together they walked toward her car.

"Do you think you could take me by my house on the way back to your place?" Sam inquired as they reached the Monte Carlo. "I just want to get my bonsai tree."

"What street is it again?"

"Sunswept Drive. It's about two miles south of downtown."

"Yeah, sure. I know where it is."

Sam had second thoughts. "You know what? It's late. I can just go by there after work tomorrow."

"No. Let's go there now," Cathy insisted.

#

Sam fished out the gift cards from his pocket and examined them while Cathy drove. He held them up and examined their fine print as the passing street lights flickered.

"Question: How in the hell am I supposed to spend $300 at a craft store?" he asked. "This was a joke, right?"

Cathy grinned but did not say anything.

"You got me," Sam admitted. "Here, you can have them. I gave up crafting in my thirties." Sam placed the gift cards on the dash. Cathy smirked and lifted them from the dash, then stuffed them back in Sam's shirt pocket.

"Listen. You're gonna walk in there and you're gonna say Nelson sent you, and that's all you need to know, okay?"

She glared at Sam. "Okay?"

Sam remained unconvinced.

89

Five minutes later, the Monte Carlo hung a left onto Sunswept Drive and crept down the pitch black street toward the reflective barricades in the distance. Cathy gripped the steering wheel, suddenly tense.

The Monte Carlo slowed to a crawl. "What are we getting into here?" Cathy asked.

"Just park over there, behind the Cadillac with the Oakland Raiders logo on the back." Cathy pulled up behind the caddy and killed the engine. A single street lamp illuminated the block, casting an ominous glow on what used to be paradise.

"Which one is yours?" Cathy asked.

"That one," Sam said, pointing at his darkened bungalow three yards away.

"And where's the..." she added.

"Over there," Sam said, pointing to the other side of the street. "It's too dark to see from here."

Sam cracked opened the passenger door. "Come with me."

"I might just stay here."

Sam turned his head to the side. "Where's your sense of adventure?"

"Fine," she said. Cathy exited the driver's side door and met Sam in front of the car. He hooked his arm into hers and guided her down the gloomy street toward the silent chaos that awaited. As they reached the barricades, Cathy stopped in her tracks.

"Jesus Fucking Christ," she gasped when she finally saw it. The crater that had once stopped at the edge of the street had now stretched out to consume the curb and five more feet of asphalt.

"Shit. It's growing," Sam observed.

"This is not good, man," Cathy muttered with her hand over her mouth. She stood on the tips of her toes. "How deep is it?"

"They said 300 feet," Sam replied. He unhooked his arm from Cathy's and scudded past the barricade.

"Where the fuck are you going?"

Sam inched slowly toward the lip of the sink hole as Cathy hugged the perimeter of the barricade, afraid to go any closer. "Maybe you shouldn't go so close to it," she said with genuine fear and concern in her voice. Sam reached the edge of the hole and looked down. He could see nothing. He was staring into a black hole, and for a moment, it consumed him.

"Sam," Cathy called out, breaking his trance. Sam turned around, struck with an epiphany.

"That's the first time you ever said my name."

That was true, and Cathy had no idea what to say next. Sam soaked in the scene, the hole, the silence. "Cathy," he finally blurted.

"Yes?"

"Oh, I just thought I should say yours too." Cathy didn't respond. Sam backed away from the sinkhole, oblivious to Cathy's fear, and turned toward his house.

"Come on," he said. "We won't be in there long." Cloaked in shadows, he couldn't see Cathy beginning to shiver at the barricade.

#

Cathy stood motionless in Sam's kitchen and glared through the back patio as Sam retrieved a puny bonsai tree from a small metal table. Through the crack in the sliding glass door Cathy could hear the swell of crickets in the backyard. She twisted her hair nervously and stared down at her overgrown toenails, certain the ground would soon open beneath her and send her forever tumbling into the black of the earth.

An eternity later, Sam wandered back into the kitchen to find Cathy shaking next to the refrigerator. He rushed over to her and grabbed her by the shoulders.

"Hey, are you okay?" Cathy's legs rattled uncontrollably against the refrigerator door, and she couldn't physically look up. "We're leaving now," Sam insisted.

Sam gripped her hand and led her out of the house as calmly as he could. As they reached her car, she slipped her hand out of his and reached into her purse for her car keys.

"Are you sure you can drive?" he asked.

"What choice do I have?" she snapped. She threw open the driver's side door and flung herself inside, slamming the door as she sat down. Sam climbed in the passenger side. Cathy cranked the engine, turned the Monte Carlo around in neck tattoo's driveway, then sped away as fast as she could from Sunswept Drive.

As the pair rode in silence, Sam realized that he had left the fucking bonsai tree in the kitchen. He stared at the orange-hued clock on Cathy's car stereo. It couldn't really be 4:34, could it? Sam stared at the numbers until the liquid in his eyes caused them to multiply. Cathy continued to drive in silence. A Jimmy Buffett song came on the radio. Sam closed his eyes, but did not fall asleep.

CHAPTER NINE

The next morning, the roaring hum of the sand blaster permeated Sam's ears with ten times more ferocity than usual. Sam tried not to let his growing discomfort and fatigue show as he prepared a tombstone for "Elizabeth Gutierrez. 1950-2015", but he was fading fast and it wasn't even close to lunch yet. Sam caught Dan glaring at him from the porch and he straightened up as much as possible. Maurice shot him a similar look as fragments of granite flew off of the deafening diamond saw, which spun at a fever pitch.

On his lunch break, Sam traipsed six blocks to where the old Ferguson Pharmacy used to be. It now housed Martha's Crafts and More, a store Sam had zero intention of entering at any other time, except today. Three hundred dollars worth of gift cards were burning a hole in his work shirt, and he wanted to call Cathy out on her bluff.

Sam pushed through the double glass doors and a cowbell rattled upon his entrance. The store was filled with everything he guessed it would be: knick-knacks, teacher supplies, art supplies, the kind of crap that grandmas love. A Mylar balloon station was plastered along one wall, and one aisle contained nothing but rubber stamps. Hundreds of the fuckers. As he angled toward the customer service desk in the center of the store, Sam passed an out-of-place biker type who stared him down as he was leaving. That was odd. When the ding of the cowbell told him that the biker had left, Sam approached the desk, where a thin woman in her fifties with a name tag that read "Nancy" stood with nothing much to do.

"Can I help you find something?" Nancy said, with a smile. Sam pulled last night's gift cards out of his pocket and hesitantly placed them on the counter. "Yeah," he said, "Nelson sent me down here."

Nancy's smile never wavered as she scooped the gift cards up from the counter. "Just a moment," she said, before disappearing through a pair of saloon-style swinging doors at the back of the store. A couple of minutes later the she reappeared carrying a plastic bag with the Martha's logo printed on the side.

"You're all set," she proclaimed with a smile as she handed the bag to Sam.

"Um, thanks," Sam responded without opening the bag. He stared at her, still slightly confused.

"Is there anything else I can help you with today?" Nancy asked with a slight forcefulness.

"I think I'm good," Sam carried the bag out of the store, setting off the cowbell once more on his way out.

Sam sat on a bench and watched as a couple of townies plodded down the street. As they passed, Sam's curiosity got the better of him. He peered into the Martha's bag. Inside he found an envelope containing two one hundred dollar bills, four twenties bills and one ten. Sam closed the bag, slightly perplexed. But then he got it.

"Crazy fucking crafters," he laughed under his breath. Sam stuck the cash into his shirt pocket and then dumped the Martha's bag in the nearest garbage bin.

#

As the day wore on, so did Sam. His second wind blew away by three o'clock and the last two hours were spent doing noticeably slow, unfocused work. This did not go unnoticed by Dan come quitting time.

"Something wrong with you, Stone?" Dan asked as he handed Sam his daily stipend.

Sam stuffed the cash into the same pocket that held his gambling winnings. "Doing just fine Dan, how are you?"

 "Maurice said you scared the shit out of him last week."

"I thought he was dead. I tried to save his life. Turns out he wasn't dead."

The phone rang in the office. It always did.

"Worry less about Maurice and worry more about Sam," Dan said. He picked up the phone. "Grave Markers."

\#

Sam's post-work mission was to go back to his house and get that goddamn bonsai tree. He figured Cathy was still upset, so it wouldn't be wise to ask her for another ride there. He felt awful about the way it had played out, and didn't really know what had happened. The car ride home had been mostly silent, and when they got back to her house, Cathy took a thirty minute shower and went to sleep. Sam had spent the next two hours sitting in the kitchen, before walking to work.

The sun was barely hanging around by the time Sam made it to Sunswept. As he crept up the street toward the barricade he spotted his neighbor Dennis loading all of his shit into the back of his El Camino. Exhausted and hungry, the last thing Sam wanted in this moment was to have a conversation with Dennis about neck tattoos.

Sam made his move about five seconds too late.

"It's bullshit!" Dennis yelled from his driveway.

Sam stopped at the curb. "What?"

"Fucking red-tagged us, man. Both of us. Half this fucking street." Dennis was on the verge of tears as he loaded a recliner into the back of his El Camino. "I fucking grew up in this house, bro."

Sam squinted at Dennis in confusion. "What are you talking about?"

"Check your fucking front door man!" Dennis exclaimed as he strapped a rope around the recliner. Sam could see the red slip of paper taped to his front door from fifty feet away. He made a bee line for it, his fear growing stronger as he got closer. When he finally reached the door the bold black letters came into focus:

DEMOLITION NOTICE.

The document contained phrases like IMMEDIATE, UNSAFE, and PERMANENTLY EVICT PREMISES. In the last paragraph, the notice listed a demolition date: July 1st. Sam's birthday.

Sam stood in disbelief. He didn't remember the notice being there the night before. When had it been posted? Still in shock, Sam unlocked his front door and entered his house. He paced the carpet room by room, soaking it in. In the living room, the brown and gray tweed couch where he masturbated and sometimes fell asleep stared back at him silently. He turned toward the dark, narrow hallway that stretched between the living room and his bedroom, its walls purposefully devoid of photos. He stepped into the hall bathroom where two incandescent bulbs burned without their shades and one lonely, broken bulb sat alone and forgotten. Sam was that bulb, at least in this moment. His last stop was the kitchen, where he found his bonsai tree sitting on the counter, right where he had left it the night before.

Stress washed over Sam. He sat down on the worn, wrinkled linoleum floor and gawked at a sea of creaky, white cabinets. He laid flat and gazed up at the popcorn ceiling. He followed the textures across the landscape, a thousand miniature hills that led to walls impossible to climb. Sam felt lost in his own hills, and he knew he should probably be packing instead of just laying here feeling depressed. He finally sat up and picked up his wallet, which had fallen out of the back pocket of his jeans.

A minute and a half later, Sam stood with the bonsai tree in the living room and took one long, last look at the place—and his stuff—fully aware that he was in fact, leaving it all to be leveled by some cruel, steel backhoe operated by some city asshole who was probably a nice guy if you got to know him. Sam did not want to get to know him. He did not want to think about this place for one more second. He did not want to rent a Budget truck and have his belongings taken to a new place, Cathy's, or wherever he ended up. He wanted nothing more in this moment than a fresh start from what was supposed to be his original fresh start. His do-over. He wanted a double do-over.

"I'll be back. I promise," Sam spoke out loud to the couch. It responded with expected silence. And with that, Sam turned and carried the bonsai tree out of the house, down the sidewalk, and away from the rental house that had been his home for the past eight years. He took one final, cursory glance at the sinkhole as the horizon killed the sun for good. He turned and saw Dennis attempting to cram a wheel barrow into the back of his overstuffed El Camino.

Dennis spotted him.

"What's that, a fucking bonsai tree?"

Sam concurred. "Yup."

"I always wanted one of those fucking things," Dennis said, lighting a cigarette.

"It was good to know you, Dennis," Sam said.

"Shit yeah, man. Sucks it had to go down like this."

Sam agreed. "Good luck to you."

"You too, man. What's your name again?"

"Sam." Sam nodded one last time then made his way down Sunswept, counting the boats in the yards one final time.

#

Cathy's house appeared empty as Sam approached it an hour and a half later. Not a single light was on in the house, and there was no sign of Cathy or the Monte Carlo. She was probably working the night shift again, Sam thought. Sam had hoped to apologize sooner rather than later. It had been almost twenty-four hours since they had spoken. But now Sam wanted nothing more than to go inside, find a soft space to lay, and sleep for as long as possible. That plan hit a major roadblock when Sam discovered that the front door was locked. With the little juice he had left in his legs, Sam hopped the chain link fence into the backyard. He lucked out—the rear door was unlocked. Sam turned on no lights as he weaved into the house and through the kitchen. Before crashing on the couch in the living room, Sam turned on the TV on top of the TV, found an infomercial, and turned the sound almost all the way down. Forty seconds later, he was asleep.

#

Sam awoke in a daze amidst a flurry of distant, angry voices coming from somewhere outside the house. He sat up and squinted at the VCR on top of the TV. It read 2:46 a.m. He stumbled to the front door and opened it, in search of the voices. He found them in the driveway. One of them belonged to Cathy, who stood next to the Monte Carlo in her work shirt

101

with her arms folded. Across the driveway, a goateed fellow leaned against a shiny, red Dodge Dakota pickup truck. He wore a hard hat by day and by night he worked as a server at a local seafood restaurant called The Crab Castle. Sam knew this because the polo shirt that he was currently wearing featured an embroidered logo that said "The Crab Castle." The sound of the screen door creaking open alerted both Cathy and Rich in the driveway.

"Who the fuck is this guy?" the man sneered when he saw Sam. "None of your damn business, Rich," Cathy said.

"This is classic, Cathy. Ollie's not in the ground a month and you've already moved some new asshole into his bedroom."

"Do I know you?" Sam asked casually from the front steps.

"No man, you don't know me," Rich responded. "Maybe the better question is 'do you know her?' Because I'm betting you don't, compadre."

Sam tried to think of the last time anyone called him compadre and he quickly determined that no one had ever called him that.

"You don't have business here anymore," Cathy snapped. "Take your ass home."

"I want my goddamn binoculars," Rich barked.

"What?" Cathy asked. "Those Bushnells in the bottom dresser drawer. Reggie gave 'em to me. I want 'em back."

Sam ducked back into the house, letting the screen door slap closed. Rich lurched closer to Cathy, slightly lowering his voice. "Where'd you meet that hippie, 1968?"

"I'm too tired for this shit, Rich. I don't want you coming around here anymore, you got no business."

"Are you fucking that guy?" Rich grabbed her forearm, trying to pull her closer. She pulled back. "Hey! Get your fuckin' hands off me!" Cathy yelped.

Sam burst back through the screen door. "Hey!" he blurted, striding with purpose toward Rich. "I got your binoculars."

Sam whipped them at Rich at fastball speed. With a THWOMP, the leather binocular case pelted Rich's shoulder, sending him flying backwards to the dirt driveway. Rich struggled to his feet, gripping his left shoulder in pain. Sam was no more than two feet away now, looking down at the man.

"Pick up your fucking binoculars and get out of here," Sam asserted. Rich maneuvered his hands through the dirt in a desperate search for the binoculars and finally retrieved them. He clutched his shoulder, never taking his eyes off of Sam. "You'll be seeing me again," Rich quavered.

"I can't wait," Sam fired back as Rich limped to his truck and sped away in defeat.

\#

Cathy entered the living room from the kitchen and handed Sam a beer on the couch. "I'm so sorry," she said.

Sam took a small sip of the beer and placed it between his legs. His fingers found the label and nervously began to peel it. "I guess I just don't know much about you," he admitted.

Cathy sat down on the couch next to him.

"Who was that guy?" Sam asked.

"That was Rich," Cathy said. "He works for the power company."

"He was wearing a Crab Castle uniform."

"He works there too," Cathy clarified. Sam was lost, confused, craving sleep.

Cathy stared at her feet, unable or unwilling to say much else, but there wasn't anything else that needed to be said. Sam reached down and pulled Cathy's hand gently toward him, turning over her forearm to see the red marks Rich had left behind.

"That son of a bitch," Sam said, his eyes red with anger. Cathy's looked at him, noticing everything. The wrinkles in his forehead. The downward tilt of his eyes, the white hairs that were slowly invading his brown beard. His full, chapped lips, dried by the Florida sun. Cathy glanced at the coffee table and spotted the bonsai tree.

"You went back for it?"

Sam nodded as his eyes floated to the wall. He let out a deep breath. "They're tearing it down," he finally admitted.

"They're doing what?"

"My house. They're demolishing it in two weeks... If that fucking hole in the ground doesn't take it first."

"That's crazy, Sam ... what are you going to do?"

Sam shook his head in defeat. "I don't know. I gotta do something."

Cathy guided her hair back behind her ears as her eyes danced around the room. "Sometimes, when a person goes through a traumatic event, they just gotta re-evaluate everything, you know? Think about your dreams – all the things you always wanted to do but never took a chance on. Like, no matter how crazy they might be. I mean, how many times in life do you get a clean slate?"

Sam realized that she was talking about herself as much as him. "So, what is the thing you always wanted to do but never took a chance on?" he asked.

Cathy smiled, surprised by the tables being turned. Her mouth opened and she turned slightly flush. She stared at Sam's guitar case leaning against the wall and angled her face toward the naked bulb that broiled in the ceiling fan above. "I wanted to sing every night in a new city," she declared.

"What's stopping you from doing that?"

Cathy shrugged. "And give up all of this?"

Sam grinned. He realized Cathy was a time bomb with no fuse - a woman who had settled as chaotically as the Florida soil she lived on. She was as ambitious as she was directionless, and Goddammit, he might be in love with her.

They shared a long silence. The house cracked and popped in the humid Florida night.

"I do have dreams," he finally admitted. She was all ears. "I just can't ever remember them." Cathy didn't appear thrilled by that answer.

"I'm going to go to sleep now," she said, rising from the couch and disappearing into the hallway. She glanced back at Sam one last time as she crossed the threshold into her bedroom.

CHAPTER 10

Sam swigged a gulp of coffee from a Stanley thermos and prepared his work station for what was looking like a light day. Two stones were on the agenda, one for each half of the schedule. Sam relished days like this. They allowed him to structure his time to do the best work possible with no rushing and no down time.

Sam was methodically hacking his chisel against a sharpening stone when he heard an unusual noise coming from the other side of the backyard—laughter. Sam looked up to find Maurice perched next to the diamond saw, an unlit Swisher Sweet between his fingers, letting loose a belly laugh for the ages. He stared at Sam as his giggles intensified. Sam turned around and glanced behind him, thinking the joke must be somewhere else, but the joke was apparently on him. Sam assumed he had entered another dimension because Maurice had never once smiled, let alone bowled over in laughter.

"What's so funny?" Sam hollered across the yard. Maurice responded with even more laughter, his aging frame bent over at the waist, his hands cupping his knees. It was insane, this laughter, maniacal. Eventually the faucet slowed to a trickle and Maurice stood back up and wiped the tears from his eyes. Sam just stared and shook his head. "Too early for this shit, man."

Maurice lit his cigar, took a satisfying first puff, then flipped on the diamond saw and cut into a piece of granite with an ear-piercing squeal.

Sam spent the first three hours of the day hand-engraving an angel graphic into a large piece of black marble. It was an expensive stone, and not a material he often had the chance to work on. He preferred it to granite. It was smoother and allowed him to chisel finer details with a smaller margin for error. Sam's energy seemed to grow as the morning rolled on, fueled by the work he was doing. He finished the black marble piece by eleven and then set out for an early lunch. Why the hell not? Dan hadn't showed up yet—par for the course. Son of a bitch never put in a full day.

#

The post office was busier than usual but Sam didn't mind waiting in line. It allowed him to meditate, reflect, and to listen to other people's conversations, which was something he had always enjoyed.

Sam pulled two-hundred dollars in cash from his shirt pocket and placed it in a Priority Mail envelope. He wrote the address, "Gary W., 402 14th St. E., Houston, TX." He paid postage with the last hundred dollar bill in his pocket and received back ninety-four dollars in change. Sam found his P.O. Box, stuck his key in, and turned the lock. It opened with a click, and Sam's eyes widened in shock as he discovered a lone envelope waiting for him inside. He had received vestigial pieces of mail throughout the years, but they had all been solicitations of the junk variety. But even those stopped coming after awhile, and the well had been completely dry for at least a year now.

Sam snatched the standard-sized white, windowless envelope from its metal casing and scrutinized it. It contained no return address or name, only his P.O. Box number. Sam held it up to the green-glowing fluorescent light above and attempted to determine what waited inside. The envelope contained a single, folded piece of paper. Anxious, he freed the captive from its wafer-thin jail and discovered a folded piece of notebook paper complete with frayed edges and a three-hole punch. Sam's heart raced as he unfolded the paper. In his hurry, the paper slipped from his hand and fell to the tile floor next to his boots, unfolding on the journey down. Sam retrieved it from the floor and could instantly make out three hand-written words. "Stop sending money," the paper read. Nothing more. It wasn't even signed.

A shell-shocked Sam rubbernecked the paper in a fog for three minutes before calmly folding it back up, sliding it back in the envelope, then sticking the envelope into his left shirt pocket. Sam stormed silently out of the post office, abandoning his PO Box with the key still stuck inside. A postal worker spotted it as Sam neared the exit and tried to tell him. "Sir, you left your key. Sir?"

Sam did not look back. Sam did not turn around. Sam kept moving. The spring in his step had been replaced by a charged motivation that would carry him back to a job he would not be able to concentrate on. Not today. Those three short words had changed everything. Sam's faded jeans whooshed as his legs carried him, one ragged boot in front of the other. As Sam neared his work site, a bigger picture had formed in his mind. He knew changes were on the horizon, but he had no idea that they had already started without him.

#

Sam could see the swirling orange and blue lights from the crest at the bottom of the hill outside the Memorial Cemetery entrance gates. An ambulance sat parked in the driveway at Dan's, parked alongside Dan's precious BMW. Sam's pace quickened. He rushed up the hill and through the tombstone-lined yard to find a shaken Dan conversing with a paramedic inside his office.

"What's going on?" Sam interrupted.

Dan looked up, white as a dove. He could barely get the words out of his mouth. "Maurice is gone."

Sam furrowed his brow and craned his neck toward the backyard, looking for Maurice. "Gone where?" The paramedic finished his chat and moved past Sam toward the backyard, where all the activity seemed to be centered.

Dan scratched at his graying temples and placed his hands on his knees, dumbfounded. "He was asleep on his lunch break and he didn't … he didn't fucking wake up. I don't know what happened."

"Jesus," Sam said. There wasn't anything else to say, really. They were both at a loss for what to do next. Dan picked up his notebook and stared at it blankly, as if the familiarity of his routine might center his emotions. Sam sat down in a metal folding chair in the office and stared at a dirty linoleum floor. He and Dan dealt with death every day – it was their business – but it had never hit so close to home.

Sam finally looked up. "What now?" he asked. Dan shook his head. He searched his notebook for some sort of guidance but couldn't even focus on its pages. He finally dropped it back on his desk before gazing out at the back yard.

"What do you have for this afternoon?" Dan inquired.

"Just that Tomlinson stone."

"They need that on Thursday," Dan said. He sucked in as much air as his beer belly would hold and then turned into a Mylar balloon with a slow leak, releasing a minute-long, squealing exhale of hot air. "Just go home, Stone. Take the rest of the day off. We'll regroup in the morning."

This was a surprise declaration and Sam wanted to make sure he heard it correctly. "Really?" he asked.

"Go home before I change my mind," Dan insisted.

Sam wasn't about to argue. He nodded, stood up and moved slowly toward the backyard. Dan called out to him. "Hey... we're going to need to make a stone for him. You think you can handle that?"

"Yes," Sam said assuredly. He stared at Dan in his squeaky office chair, his face flush with stress, wearing that same tired polo shirt with the uneven collar that he wore three times a week. He was a mess.

"You okay?" Sam asked, genuinely concerned.

Dan nodded, his eyes glazing over. "I was just thinking about my dad." It was the first personal thing Dan had shared with Sam in their entire eight-year relationship. Sam felt honored. "I bet he was a great guy," Sam said before turning and wandering into the back yard.

Sam stopped on the porch and peered out at the work area. At the edge of the yard, two funeral home lackeys in black suits and blue latex gloves struggled to slide Maurice's heavy, sun-beaten body off the slab of granite and onto a waiting stretcher. Sam stepped off the porch and shuffled closer, his curiosity leading the way. The sight of the limp corpse didn't make him wince or gag, but he did wonder why Maurice had been laughing at him earlier. He would never know now, but it didn't really matter. Two pasty white men were going to cart him into a waiting hearse and transport his body less than two hundred yards to the funeral home down the street where they would vacuum out his organs and stuff him into a steel box for the princely sum of $10,000. What a racket, Sam thought.

Sam's proximity must have irked one of the funeral home jerks, who looked up at Sam mid-struggle. "Can you give us a hand here?" Sam had no idea if he was serious. He was.

"I don't have any of those gloves," Sam muttered. The funeral home jerk instantly produced a pair of latex gloves from his inner suit pocket and flung them at Sam. They landed on

113

Sam's shoulder, sending a puff of blue powder into the air. Sam glanced back toward the house and saw Dan staring at him from the porch. Sam was too deep into the pool at this point, so he pulled on the impossibly tight gloves and proceeded to help lift Maurice's body onto the oversized gurney.

"We can take it from here," the funeral home dickbag shrilled. "You can keep the gloves." The other funeral home asshole laughed—funeral home humor. Sam watched the men wheel the gurney toward a waiting hearse that had its back doors wide open. The legs on the gurney collapsed with a loud click and the back end of the hearse sunk slightly as Maurice's oversized corpse rolled inside. Sam turned back toward the office, but Dan was no longer standing there.

After the hearse sped away, Sam passed by the diamond saw that Maurice had so masterfully operated for all those years. Sam had never stood this close to it, Maurice had never let him. He scanned the impressive, terrifying machine. He always figured if Maurice was going to die on the job, it would be in the machine, not near it. Sam never wished anything bad on Maurice, but he did wonder what it would look like if someone lost an arm in that thing. He wasn't about to find out now. A few feet away, Sam spotted the grave markers he had completed the day before. He shuffled over to inspect them. That's when he saw it.

"Gutierez."

Sam scratched his eyebrows as he read the word a dozen times letter by letter. Something wasn't right, but he couldn't nail it down. The truth finally hit him and Sam's face became a sheet.

"GUTIEREZ."

Sam's fingers tunneled through his hair and he began to sweat, his heart jumping as he ran through a laundry list of possible explanations: Maybe they just spell it with one "r," he thought. Maybe it's just an unconventional spelling. Maybe the mistake was on the paperwork. That might save his ass. Sam checked the paperwork attached to the stone. "Gutierrez."

"FUCK," Sam blurted to no one. "Fuck shit fuck."

He stared at the stone as if fixating on it would somehow change it. This was bad. Bad, bad, bad. The sweat from his forehead raced down his cheeks. Sam had made minor mistakes on grave markers before, but he had never completely butchered a stone. In eight years—hundreds of stones, dozens of nationalities—he had never once misspelled someone's name. Not. One. Time.

And yet, there was no mistaking it: the stone was ruined. A $4,000 piece of stunning black marble was completely, irreversibly fucked. He surmised Dan hadn't seen it yet. If he had, he hadn't spotted the error. But he would. It would only be a matter of time before the stone was delivered to the cemetery—to the family—and he would be on the hook for it. He knew the cost to replace it would come out of his pay. Every last penny of it.

Sam did the calculations in his head. He would lose two months pay, maybe three. He would work for free the entire summer to make up for it. Three long months in the brutal Florida humidity, slaving over marble and granite with a chisel and mallet, for zero pay.

"Stop sending money."

The words suddenly replayed in Sam's mind, as the other shit storm brewing in his life flew back to the forefront.

Sam took a deep breath and glanced back at the house. He realized in that moment that he was about to walk away from Dan's Grave Markers for the last time.

Sam snuck back to his station and grabbed his trusty chisel and mallet. He had no reason to do so. The tools belonged to Dan, but Sam attached real emotion to them. They were an extension of his hands and arms, and they had served him well over the last eight years. With these three pieces of rubber, wood and metal he had been able to help grieving families deal with their grief, and though he rarely if ever met them, he believed that he made a difference. Whether or not it was true, he left believing it.

Sam slunk away from Dan's in a bit of a daze. He glanced over his shoulder one last time as he made his way down the hilly decline. With his mallet and chisel in hand, he could've been a serial killer stalking his prey by daylight, but he was just Sam. A man with no house, no job, and nowhere to send his money.

CHAPTER 11

As much as Cathy loathed the havoc of the night shift at RJ's, the afternoon crowd was an equally-imposing beast, and today's crop was among the worst. A bus between Miami and Atlanta had deposited three dozen gamble-happy senior citizens into the arcade. Cathy's patience for technology-challenged, hearing-impaired token droppers was growing thin. To make matters worse, the arcade was short staffed until seven, meaning Cathy was alone at the front, selling tokens to a never-ending throng of unwelcome septuagenarians.

At some point, the money in Cathy's till reached the tipping point. Concerned with the overflow of cash she had on hand, Cathy picked up a walkie-talkie and signaled backup. "Hey Andrew, I need to make a cash drop and we're low on tokens."

A filtered voice replied, "I'll be up there as soon as I can, the video feed just went out."

A strange excuse, Cathy thought. The camera systems were hard-wired with battery back-ups, and RJ's spent a shitload to make sure they could see every nook and cranny in the place at all times. The video feed couldn't just "go out." Cathy set the walkie-talkie down and came face-to-face with an old woman in khaki shorts who couldn't find the bathroom.

Andrew showed up three minutes later. He was twenty-nine years old, and all of five-foot two.

"Is the feed still down?" Cathy asked. But Andrew was clearly not fucking around. "I don't know what's going on," the anxious, sweaty manager fumed. "Lester is on his way. Go make your drop and hurry back."

"I'm going to show this lady where the bathroom is on the way," Cathy said.

"Fine. Just hurry," Andrew snarled. Cathy escorted the old woman through the arcade and into a long, narrow hallway at the back of the arcade. "Here you go," she said, leaving the old woman outside the women's bathroom. She then headed for the cash office, a small, stainless steel-enforced room with a metal door and a bank-style automated drawer. Cathy pushed a glowing intercom button and waited. A metal peephole slid open and a pair of anonymous eyes stared back. She spoke into a small condenser microphone.

"Hey, Darnell. Making a drop and I need a two boxes of tokens." A few seconds later, she heard three clicking sounds, and the steel drawer slid toward her. She placed a vinyl bank bag into the drawer and waited. The drawer half-closed and stopped. The eyes in the peephole squinted.

The lights in the arcade flickered and went dark. A chorus of angry senior citizens cried foul from the game room, but their outbursts were soon drowned out by the sudden, overpowering rush of armed DEA agents exploding into the arcade through the front door.

"EVERYONE DOWN ON THE GROUND!" This request was met by a heart attack and two strokes while the remaining senior citizens hit the floor as quickly as their frail hips would allow.

The chaos in the front could be heard from the cash office. Cathy became a statue as men in tactical gear flooded into the arcade. BOOM! BOOM! BOOM! Cathy jumped as a battering ram pummeled into the back door just feet from her. These fuckers had the place surrounded. Stunned by the vibrations, Cathy fell backwards onto the carpet outside the cash office. With agents filling the arcade and the back door one battering ram away from bursting open, Cathy found her feet and stum-

bled silently into a nearby storage closet, locking it before trip-
ping forward. She stabbed her hands into darkness and found a
pull-string which illuminated a single, 60-watt bulb overhead.
Dozens of broken and discarded slot machines and various
pieces of arcade equipment surrounded her. She spotted an escape route—a metal door on the far wall behind some dusty
cash registers.

The noise from the arcade intensified. The mayhem seemed
to be growing closer by the second. Cathy advanced quickly and
quietly toward her escape route. She unlatched the lock at the
top, pressed the door handle down and leaned her shoulder into
it, but it didn't budge.

"Fuck!" she cried under her breath. She rammed it three
more times and kicked it, to no avail. "Goddamit, come on!"
Cathy yelled, a bit too loudly. She heard voices approaching the
closet. It was only then that Cathy realized that there was also a
latch at the bottom of the door. She twisted the rusty bottom
latch until it loosened upwards with a metallic screech. She
leaned against the door handle one more time and it flew open,
sending her crashing into no man's land.

Cathy now found herself in a cramped, three-foot-wide corridor that connected the arcade to the 7-Eleven next door. It
was a place where nothing good ever happened. Earlier in the
winter, a homeless man was found dead underneath a blanket of

cardboard—but this hall of doom was Cathy's saving grace right now, and quite possibly the only thing keeping her from going to jail.

Cathy ranged up and down the dim hall but quickly determined that neither end had an exit. Panicked, Cathy considered lying down and covering herself with empty boxes that were littered with rat feces, but then she saw it: a sliver of light in the distance. Another door was hidden behind a stack of abandoned milk cartons. Cathy raced toward it like a lost soul seeking eternity. Locks be damned, Cathy rammed the door with 115 pounds of muscle behind her.

Cathy landed face down on the other side of the door and soon discovered she was lying in the dull, fluorescent glow of the 7-Eleven stockroom. This was confirmed when Cathy climbed to her feet and discovered a stack of boxes labeled "Slurpee." She then discovered something else—a bank bag on a dirty tile floor with the RJ's Game Zone logo on it. It took a moment for Cathy to register its origins, but she soon realized that she must have held onto the drop bag when the raid happened. Cathy kneeled down and quickly unzipped the pouch. Holy shit. Yup. That was her bag alright, stuffed with cash. "Holy shit," Cathy whispered, glancing back at the corridor then toward the entrance to the 7-Eleven.

Cathy ducked through the stock room door and entered the 7-Eleven as nonchalantly as anyone with a bag of money stuffed down the front of their shirt possibly could. Once inside, Cathy did what anyone does in a 7-Eleven: she bought two taquitos and a Slurpee and then loafed into the parking lot, catching a quick glimpse of the madness next door in her peripheral vision. Cathy never turned her eyes fully to the scene—fear of being recognized prevented that—but as she slunk into her car, she glanced in her rear view mirror to see a row of senior citizens lined up on the curb, their prune-like skin baking in the sweltering Florida heat. Cathy saw a S.W.A.T. member dragging Andrew out in handcuffs, his arms flailing and his mouth moving. She let out a deep, much-needed breath and slid her key into the ignition. She had never heard a more beautiful sound than the Monte Carlo's engine turning over.

#

As Sam paced through sun-drenched streets en route to Cathy's house, he pulled the letter from his pocket and unfolded it again. "Stop sending money." The hand-written, black lettering seemed to appear darker under natural light than beneath the fluorescent lights in the post office. It was as if the letter was hammering the point home.

"Stop sending money," Sam finally said out loud as his feet carried him in wide, three-foot strides. Anger eating away at

123

him, Sam stopped near a bridge that overlooked shoddy rental houses lining a sad, man-made stream. He wadded the letter and the envelope into his fists and hurled the paper snowball as far into the water as he could. A breeze caught the wad and stopped it short of the water's edge, plopping the crumpled document on the concrete lip of the water. Of course that's where it landed, Sam thought. Sam began to sink, and the longer he stared at it, the more he came to realize that he was not unlike the scrunched paper on the water's edge below. He had jumped the bridge only to land inches from his own estuary, and goddammit, he didn't even know how to swim.

"Stop sending money."

Still reeling, Sam halted outside an auto parts store and found the last working pay phone in Western Florida. Three quarters and eleven rings later, Sam listened to the same voice mail he had heard when he'd called from Cathy's cell phone. "Hey, this is Gary. Leave a message." This time around, Sam let him have it.

"Gary, why don't you answer your fucking phone, man? I got your fucking letter. What the hell does 'stop sending money' mean? I'm kind of at a loss here. I've been sending money for seven years. What happened that would cause me to stop now? Are you there? Gary? Pick up the phone Gary. I swear, if this is just you—"

BEEP.

Sam slammed the receiver down so hard that it shattered into pieces on the sidewalk below him. A large man in a tan Dickies work shirt flopped out of the auto parts store as Sam skidded away.

"What the fuck are you doing, man? Hey!"

The man chugged to the sidewalk but discovered Sam's pace was too quick for him. He glared at the phone, in pieces at his feet. "Fuckin' asshole!" he yelled after Sam.

Sam entered Cathy's house to find a chaotic, ransacked scene. The house was a tornado of scattered clothing, trash bags and toiletries, but there was no sign of Cathy.

"Hello?" Sam called out. He glanced in the kitchen, but Cathy wasn't there. He angled back through the living room and into the hall. Her bedroom door was slightly ajar. "Cathy?" Sam asked, pushing the door open slowly. Inside, he found Cathy standing next to her bed, maniacally stuffing items into a vintage Samsonite suitcase. She whipped around, startled.

"You scared the shit out of me!"

Sam's face filled with confusion. "What's happening here?"
"I'm leaving."

"You're leaving? Where are you going?"

Cathy pushed down hard on a pile of clothing and attempted to close the suitcase lid, but her unmentionables squeezed out of one side. Undeterred, she tried again. "West," she said, finally snapping the suitcase closed. She reached down and picked up her tattered guitar case and hoisted it up onto the bed. "To California."

"Why? What happened?"

"You were right, Sam. I need to follow my dreams."

Sam knew there had to be more to the story, but there was no time to push. Cathy would be out the door in seconds flat. She rocketed past him into the bathroom and began to toss the contents of her medicine cabinet into a plastic bag. She turned to leave the bathroom and found Sam standing in her way.

"What are you doing?" she asked. Sam's eyes searched for hers, but couldn't make contact. She stared at his tanned forearms, her mind racing fast enough to keep her heart from thumping. "I have to go Sam, don't do this." Cathy brushed past Sam into the bedroom and gathered her luggage.

"Take me with you," Sam blurted. Cathy stopped in the middle of the room and set her bags down on the floor.

"What?"

"I have no house. I have no job. There's nothing for me here anymore."

"What happened to your job?" she asked, suddenly concerned.

"What happened to *your* job?" Sam snapped back. Neither seemed to have the right answer.

"Look, I have some business in Texas," Sam said, after a long silence. "Can you take me there?"

"What's in Texas?"

"Just something I need to do," Sam said, his voice almost breaking.

Cathy stared at Sam, searching for the real person behind his eyes. "What is this thing that we're doing?" she asked. Sam knew what she meant, but he didn't know how to answer her. He just shook his head and said, "Traveling."

Cathy laughed and bit her bottom lip. "Okay," she said. Sam retrieved Cathy's bags from the floor. "You don't have to do that," she insisted, but Sam didn't listen to her. He carried the bags out of the room toward the front door. Chivalry was not dead.

Sam stuffed Cathy's bags into the Monte Carlo. He then went inside to retrieve his own belongings—the sleeping bag, his grandfather's guitar, his records and his bonsai tree. Sam carried them toward the door.

"You ready?" he asked. Cathy nodded, then hesitated as they reached the threshold.

"Just a minute," she said, retreating slowly through the living room toward the hallway. She took a left in the hall and Sam

127

knew instantly where she was going. He set his bags down and waited.

Cathy stopped outside of Ollie's room and took a long look at the door before finding the courage to enter. She finally turned the knob and stepped into a raging river of memories from a world that she no longer lived in. Every item in the room brought back a recollection of her son – some so joyous and strong she couldn't believe how easily they were lost, and one so intensely sad she could do nothing but completely close herself off from it. It was a room filled with things that didn't belong to anyone anymore, just the specter of a boy who would never catch grasshoppers in a field by day or count the stars again at night. Faced with goodbye, Cathy lied down on Ollie's bed one last time and closed her eyes.

CHAPTER 12

Alan Walker could barely keep his eyes open. He stood, zombie-like, at the sink outside of Surgery Room 2. Regulations called for three continuous minutes of hand-washing with a coarse sponge from his elbows down to his fingernails, but the warm, soapy water was lulling him to sleep. Alan worked the sponge into a thick lather as a digital timer counted down the minutes. A piercing BEEP at the end of the countdown acted as Alan's alarm clock. He opened his eyes, dried his hands, retrieved a surgical mask and gloves from a wall-mounted dispenser, and then straggled into the operating room with dazed purpose.

A handful of nurses and an anesthesiologist waited. A patient may or may not have been there too—it was hard to say.

Alan squinted as he approached the blinding, suffocating light above the operating table where—oh, there she was—a young woman lay unconscious on her back, prepped for surgery. It was only in this brief moment, under the glow of that harsh yellow light, that Alan questioned his ability to do his job. The rational part of his brain, which was asleep, told him to admit his fatigue and tap out. Unfortunately, the side of his brain which contained the doctor's ego and pride was wide awake and ready to tell anyone who stood in his way to *fuck off, I got this*. A more complicated surgery might have scared the pride away, but not this one. Not a standard, run-of-the-mill, non-laparoscopic appendectomy. Alan could do this surgery in his fucking sleep, and he was about to.

"Where are we at?" Alan asked the anesthesiologist.

"Intubated. Full muscle relaxation," he responded.

"Okay. Let's do this," Alan slurred. The nurse to his right handed him a scalpel. Alan's eyes temporarily lost focus in the spotlight that shined on the patient's open abdomen. Alan's heels tipped back slightly as his knees threatened to give out, but he somehow regained his balance. The nurse across from him noticed and made eye contact with the head RN.

"Everything OK, doctor?" she asked. Alan forged ahead, his focus blurry.

"Incision over McBurney's Point," Alan said before slowly cutting a three-inch opening in the patient's abdomen. Alan took a deep breath, his legs betraying him again. He shifted his weight from one leg to the other. "Opening the uh... the abdominal wall."

After cutting through the external and internal oblique muscles, Alan blacked out for an indeterminate amount of time. Somehow, his eyes remained open during the blackout and he did not lose his balance, but he had reached the point where he was in effect, "sleep surgerying." A hot buzzing in his nerves sent waves of electricity to his limbs and fingertips. He could feel the vibration working its way into his face as his chin and nose began to tingle. He was still not conscious at this point, operating only on muscle memory.

As Alan cut through the peritoneum, the hearing in his right ear went out and the voices of the nurses in the room became distant echoes.

"Appendix is ligated and diverted," Alan declared as he let out what seemed like his last waking breath. "Turning the stump toward ... turning toward the cecum."

Twelve minutes later, the surgery was over. Somehow, Alan had managed to complete it without killing the patient. He had no memory of stitching up the young woman, or of changing into his street clothes, or of walking from the hospital to his car, but he remembered getting in and starting it. Alan cranked the engine on his white 2003 BMW 9 Series—his pride and joy. He pulled out of the parking lot, convinced that it was somewhere between seven and nine in the morning. It was, in fact, four in the afternoon. Alan stopped at a red light near the hospital and pulled out his cell phone.

"Hey. I'm on my way. Be there in thirty minutes," he said.

The light turned green and Alan hit the accelerator. He felt his grip on the wheel tighten as he merged onto Highway 59, a dirty, congested stretch of Houston blanketed by overpasses and billboards for DWI lawyers and vasectomy reversals. As the white lines of the highway jousted toward him, Alan felt himself giving in to the call of unconsciousness, until the blast of a tailgating eighteen-wheeler's air horn jolted him awake—wide awake—for a moment. Alan checked his speedometer. He was driving thirty miles per hour on a highway with a speed limit of seventy. As cars horns blared and vehicles passed him on both sides, Alan stomped the accelerator and the BMW responded with two hundred fifty-five horses, shooting him back into the flow of traffic within seconds. Alan changed lanes as the Interstate 10 exit approached. He felt relieved to have finally reached the halfway point to his modest suburban home on the outskirts of Bayville.

The next twenty minutes were more or less a blur as Alan routinely drifted outside the far right lane and onto the painted white rumble strips designed to inform him that he was driving off the road. Every time he hit the strip, he jerked back to the left, as he struggled to stay awake. Alan finally made it off the highway and back onto the low-key comfort of surface streets. From the underpass, it was a short three-mile jaunt down a two-lane road to his home, the largest on the cul-de-sac. As the BMW laid rubber to that quiet asphalt, Alan relaxed, knowing that he was in the home stretch.

That's when his eyes closed.

CHAPTER 13

The plan was to get the hell out of Escapade, cut north on Interstate 75 through Gainesville and be halfway to Tallahassee by dinner time, but four hours into the journey Sam and Cathy had traveled scarcely ninety six miles. Traffic on the highway was bumper-to-bumper, and the two screaming ambulances that flew down the service road were signs of definite trouble ahead. The Monte Carlo was packed so tightly that the rear window wasn't even visible, forcing Sam to stick his neck out of the passenger window to see how far back the traffic stretched.

"I don't see any cars moving anywhere," Sam reported, his face leaning into the golden sun. He rubbed his right ear and removed a thick, waxy substance from it. He curled it up into a ball with his fingers and dropped it onto the highway. A thin layer of sweat pooled on Cathy's face as the sun bounced off the asphalt, throwing waves of heat into the car. The Monte Carlo had 214,000 miles on the odometer but was still as reliable as ever, though it did not come equipped with the luxuries of modern living, namely air conditioning.

Cathy scanned the car radio in search of a traffic report but came up empty. She finally rested the dial on a classic country station playing Jimmy Buffett's "Come Monday." Cathy wiped the sweat from her face and tapped her fingers on the steering wheel as Jimmy "headed up to San Francisco." Cathy's eyes scanned the floorboard and landed on the stack of records laying underneath Sam's feet.

"Why do you have all those records when you don't even have anything to play 'em on?" Cathy asked.

"They were my grandfather's," Sam explained. "I plan on listening to them someday."

"Wait—you've never played 'em?"

"Never had anything to play them on."

"That's weird," Cathy said, trying to hold a burst of laughter. "How long have you been toting those things around?"

Sam considered the question long and hard. "I don't remember," he finally muttered. He wasn't lying. The answer seemed good enough for Cathy.

"Which ones you got, anyway?" Cathy asked. Sam reached down between his legs and pulled them out one at a time.

"Let's see … Willie Nelson. *Shotgun Willie*. I like the cover on this one." Sam held it up. "It's got Willie's face in both barrels of a shotgun."

"I see that."

"This one with the man on the horse—Jerry Jeff Walker, *Ridin' High*. Looks interesting. There's a song called "Pissin' in the Wind" on it. I wonder what that's about."

"You know, they usually put a sheet of paper in there with the lyrics, if you were really curious," Cathy half-joked. Sam's eyes narrowed as he studied the gatefold. "That's good info. I might have to check that out."

"What's the blue one?" Cathy asked.

Sam slid the first two records down between his legs and retrieved the last one. Its ring-worn cover featured a man sitting on a bale of hay with an army of bales surrounding him. At the top, in simple white typeset, was the name …

"John Prine." Sam glanced at the back cover, then quickly turned it back over to the front. "They must all be good if my grandfather left them to me," he said as the Jimmy Buffett song ended and silence filled the car.

"Was he nice?" Cathy asked. "Your grandpa."

"He was a simple man, a people person," Sam said, staring out the passenger window. "He owned a sand and gravel business and he liked to chew Red Man. My grandmother left him and then he found God. That's about all I know."

"Wonder why she left him?" Cathy inquired.

Sam shrugged. "I never asked him."

Cathy studied Sam. "So, why don't you drive?" she said.

"I don't have a valid license," Sam said. It was a pithy excuse, but true. Sam glanced at Cathy. She was sun-soaked, fatigued. The Monte Carlo hadn't moved an inch in 15 minutes. The highway was a parking lot and the car was an oven. Any hint of a breeze was like God himself waving a collapsible Japanese fan in their direction. "I'm sorry I'm no help," Sam apologized. They both stared out at the sea of motionless cars in front of them.

"So much for making it to Alabama by sundown," Sam quipped.

Cathy's mind wandered. "I know someone in Tallahassee," she said, "but I haven't talked to her in a few years."

"Can you call her?"

Cathy picked up her cell phone, an old flip-style number. "I need to buy another card for this stupid pay-by-the-minute phone."

Cathy's face turned extra serious, maybe even a little sullen. Her eyes squinted as the late afternoon sun streaked through the windshield so brightly it seemed like the dash might catch on fire.

As quickly as the traffic had halted, the never-ending stretch of cars suddenly crept ahead. The chain reaction took a couple of minutes to reach the Monte Carlo, but when it did, Cathy finally lifted her foot off of the brake pedal and pressed it against the accelerator. It was a tiny victory, but moving forward at all felt damn good.

Traffic remained stop-and-start for the next few miles, but as they neared a curve in the distance, flashing lights came into view. Past that point, cars picked up speed, as if fleeing some awful scene. As Sam and Cathy approached the oscillating red and green luminaries, an accident scene appeared. A lone motorcycle lay mangled against a concrete center divider in the middle of a construction zone. Shards of metal and plastic littered the asphalt near the bike.

"Jesus," Cathy said. The Monte Carlo slowly rolled past the fallen motorcycle, where a white sheet covered a man's body on the interstate shoulder. His legs jutted out beyond the red-streaked sheet, his jeans ripped and one boot missing. A pair of EMTs stood near the body and spoke to a police officer. As the scene faded into her rear view mirror, Cathy glanced over at Sam, who stared sharply in the opposite direction.

"Did you see that?" she asked, the Monte Carlo reaching a forty miles per hour clip that felt like ninety under the circumstances. Sam kept his head angled away from the inside of the highway.

"I missed it," he said.

#

The Monte Carlo rolled into the Tallahassee around seven o'clock and its passengers were sun-sick and starving. Sam and Cathy snaked through downtown in search of some address that Cathy thought she remembered but wasn't quite sure about. Sam gazed out of his window at the government buildings and retail shops that lined the streets of the Florida capital. Downtown wasn't exactly a ghost town after hours, but it certainly lacked the hustle and bustle of the work day. Business types stood outside hip bars perfect for happy hours and first dates, but with the college campus cleared for the summer, the vibe was decidedly relaxed.

Cathy's face turned sickly as they drove down a tree-lined avenue. "All these live oaks make me want to puke," she said. The foliage didn't seem to have the same effect on Sam, who felt refreshed by the welcome wind funneling through the car.

"George Clinton is from Tallahassee," Sam said, proud of his random factoid, but Cathy wasn't paying attention.

"Hawthorne Street? I think this is it," she said, hanging a right down a suburban street lined with upper middle class homes. Per usual, Sam set out to count the number of boats parked in yards but was disappointed to find none in the neighborhood.

The Monte Carlo parked in front of a white Tudor-style house with a yard so immaculate the only thing missing was a sign that said "Please don't walk on the grass." Cathy killed the engine and sat idle for several moments as she stared at the house. She looked over at Sam. "Did you say something about Bill Clinton?"

Sam shook his head and peeped at the idyllic house in the distance.

"I'm fucking starving," he said before immediately apologizing. "Sorry, I get grumpy when I'm hungry. Are we going in?"

Cathy stared at the house. "So here's the thing … this is my sister's house."

Sam lit up. "I didn't know you had a sister," he said, his interest piqued.

"I do. I have a sister," Cathy said. She let out a deep breath. "We should probably leave."

"Why?" Sam asked. Cathy sat still, meditating for another thirty seconds before abruptly abandoning the car and making a bee line for the house.

"Oh. Okay," Sam said, clambering out and giving chase. By the time he caught up with Cathy, she had already knocked on the front door.

"Cathy? Oh my God," a female voice said a moment later. "I wasn't expecting you." Sam looked up at Norah, mid forties, the slightly older, more successful version of Cathy. The sisters shared the same blonde hair and striking features, but were night and day in pretty much every other facet of their appearance. Norah's red cardigan perfectly draped over a white silk blouse from Macy's or Bloomingdale's or wherever successful women shopped these days. Cathy wore a tank top over a bra, and she probably couldn't tell you where she got either of them.

"We were just driving through," Cathy said, looking back. "This is Sam. Sam, this is Norah." Norah scanned Sam and flashed a courtesy smile, anxiety written all over her face.

"Please, come in," Norah said, clearly uncomfortable. "We were just sitting down for dinner." Norah held the front door open and Cathy signaled Sam to take the lead. He obliged, moving through the threshold with Cathy trailing behind a moment later. As Sam walked down a narrow hallway, Norah stopped Cathy in the foyer.

"Cathy?" she whispered. "I just wanted to say that I am so sorry about not coming to Ollie's service. It was sweeps week. I couldn't get away. I feel terrible." Norah pulled her in for a hug which Cathy had no choice but to accept. The long, uncomfortable embrace finally ended as Cathy pulled back.

"It's okay," Cathy said. "I know how important your career is to you." Cathy offered a forced smile. "But thank you for the flower spray. It was stunning." Cathy burst down the hall toward the kitchen in the distance. Norah stood stunned, completely unprepared for the hurricane that had just blown ashore.

Sam and Cathy soon found themselves sitting at a large oak table in a formal dining room with all the upper middle class accoutrements. Cathy poked at a small dinner salad. Sam's carrot food sat uneaten in front of him. He could easily polish off three burgers in ten minutes, but he'd be goddamned before he ate any lettuce.

Across from Sam sat Josh, Norah's husband, an all-around okay but completely non-descript white dude in his forties wearing a striped Van Heusen dress shirt. Norah sat next to him, but she might as well have been on the other side of the room. At the end of the table, in the king's seat, sat their nine-year-old son Grayson—the spitting image of Josh. Sam watched jealously as Josh took a bite of salmon.

"I'm sorry there's not enough fish," Norah apologized. "We weren't expecting company." She looked at her husband, who flashed a supportive smile.

"It's fine," Cathy retorted. "I don't eat fish."

"I eat fish," Sam said.

"You can have mine," Grayson said, giving the stink-eye to his salmon as if it might come back to life and jump off his plate.

"Eat your fish, Grayson," Norah demanded, but Grayson just stared at it. Josh took a long drink of iced tea and smiled at Sam. They were complete opposites, looks-wise, and probably in every other imaginable way.

"So how did you two meet?" Josh asked, cutting the tension like someone who cut tension for a living.

Sam glanced at Cathy then back at Josh. "We met in the cemetery."

"The cemetery?" Josh cried out, legitimately enthralled. "That's interesting!" Josh robotically winked at Grayson as if he should be in on some kind of inside joke. Grayson responded with a blank stare. Josh beamed at Sam. "What do you do for a living, Stan?"

All that Sam could think about was Maurice's dead body baking out in the Florida sun on that smooth slab of granite.

Also, food. Any kind of food. "I do tombstone etchings," he said, his eyes shifting to Cathy. "That's actually how I met—"

"He etched the tombstone of my dead son," Cathy said bluntly, staring daggers at Norah.

Grayson's eyes popped open as Norah's fork clanked against her plate. "Grayson, you can be excused," Norah said.

"Can I stay?" Grayson asked for the first time ever.

"Grayson, go to your room!" Norah insisted. Grayson hemmed and hawed and then stood up and exited the dining room, taking one last look at over his shoulder as he traversed a solid oak staircase.

"That's a good kid you've got there," Sam said, trying anything to divert his mind away from his appetite. His stomach growled.

"We like him," Josh said, all smiles.

As the silence grew, the tension returned like a fog rolling in from all directions, filling the room with a thick mist of discomfort. If there was ever a moment ripe for a subject change, this would be it.

"I'm a brand manager for a major frozen foods company," Josh blurted out, just in time. He glanced over at Norah, who wouldn't even look at him. Josh's smile grew as wide as Texas. "Sam, have you ever had Rotino's Pizza Pouches?"

Sam lit up like the Rockefeller Plaza Christmas tree. "Uh, yeah. Pepperoni Blasters? I eat those things like two bags at a time."

"Why did you come here?" Norah asked Cathy, calmly but seriously, as the room split into two very different conversations.

Cathy glared at her sister. "I thought I wanted to see you but as soon as I saw you I realized I didn't want to see you." A solid right hook, and Norah's face dropped.

"I was the driving force behind the re-design of the Pepperoni Blasters packaging," Josh said to Sam, beaming with pride. "If you compare the new bag to the old one, the pouches now appear twenty-two percent larger."

Sam radiated as if warmed by a revelation. "They do look larger."

"Well here's the thing, Sam," Josh added. "They're actually smaller."

Sam's eyes opened wide. "Shut the fuck up! I'm sorry, I curse when I'm surprised, or hungry."

Norah stared daggers at Cathy. "You have some nerve coming here and bringing this… hostility."

"Pardon the hostility, sis. Maybe you should've come to your nephew's funeral."

145

"I can't just ..." Norah grew agitated. "I'm the number two meteorologist in this market!"

Sam's eyes found the door to the kitchen. "Hey, do you have any here?" he asked Josh.

Josh threw down his napkin. "I have a freezer full of the things!"

Sam couldn't believe his ears. The luck!

"You never do miss a chance to let anyone know how important you are," Cathy fired at Norah. "I mean, what would people do if they didn't have you to tell them about the weather? How would they ever find out the day's temperature?"

"Enough!" Norah screamed. She stood up with her plate balanced precariously on her porcelain fingertips. She considered her options — throw it at Cathy, slam it against the wall, or just set it back down. And there it stayed, for a full minute, all eyes in the room drawn to it like a circus trick.

"I'm not going to let you do this to me," Norah wailed, on the verge of a breakdown. "Not again, Cathy. You came here to push your guilt onto me. You want me to feel bad for my success. Bad for having the life that you wanted. Well, guess what? I don't feel bad and I don't feel guilty. Do you want to know why? Because I made good choices. And this thing that exists between us, whatever you want to call it—it's not a relationship. It hasn't been a relationship since we were teenagers. You call and you come around when it's crisis time and you need something. It's always a car fire with you, Cathy. Don't you think I want a relationship with my sister that isn't based solely on broken down relationships and stretches of unemployment and boyfriends who left you stranded on the side of the road in Orlando?" Norah eyed Sam. "And this guy, he seems like a very nice fellow. But how many different versions of this guy are you going to bring here?"

Sam studied Cathy, stunned by her sister's soliloquy.

Norah continued: "I would love nothing more than for you to call me up on a Sunday afternoon and just say 'Hey Norah, how are you? How are things going? Do you want to go get ice cream later?' But it's never been that way and it never will be because your life doesn't work that way. You're a living, breathing, walking crisis. And I'm sorry that your son died. I wish I had known him. I wish I could've been there. But goddammit, Cathy, I couldn't take another crisis!"

And with that, Norah swung her hand outward, sending her plate flying into the crown molding and smashing into a million pieces. It was almost an afterthought—a period instead of an exclamation mark. Norah stared at her hand in disbelief and then sat back down. Silent and calm, but clearly shaken.

Josh reached over and touched the top of Norah's hand. Sam snapped from his hunger daze as Cathy slowly rose from her seat and wiped her face with her napkin.

"You're right, Norah. I'm a car fire," she said. She nudged Sam, who took her cue and stood up.

"Yeah, we should probably head out," Sam said, attempting to salvage some sense of normalcy. Sam extended his hand and Josh shook it firmly.

"You're a good guy, Scott," Josh said.

"Thanks, man," Sam replied, completely okay with the name flub.

Cathy rumbled, unblinking, past her sister into the hallway. Norah's nerves had calmed a bit by now. "Cathy, wait," she called out. "I'm sorry."

Sam stopped to help pick up the broken shards. "Please don't hurt yourself," Norah pled. "We can clean up."

"It's really no problem," Sam insisted, retrieving each piece from the floor, using his finger and thumb to pinch even the tiniest shards without a single piece cutting him. He offered a smile to Norah who flashed one back out of courtesy.

By the time Sam finished picking up the pieces, Cathy had reached the front door. She opened it and turned back around. "I'm moving to California," she said. "I don't know if I'll see you again." And with that, Cathy vanished through the door and out of her sister's house.

Sam lingered behind for a moment as he gazed at Norah in the hallway. "Thank you for offering me salad," he said.

CHAPTER 14

Cathy gripped the steering wheel and glared through a grimy, bug-covered windshield while the Monte Carlo's tread-bare tires ka-thumped over warm Tallahassee asphalt. Her body was in the driver's seat, but Sam could tell her mind was somewhere else entirely.

"Are you OK?" he asked.

"I'm fine," Cathy said through gritted teeth. The pair drove in silence another few miles until Sam broke it with—

"I've got a brother."

Cathy looked over, intrigued.

"You guys get along?" she asked. Sam thought about the best way to phrase it, but all he could come up with was: "We used to. He's just an asshole now."

Cathy agreed. "Were you a black sheep, too?"

"Yeah," Sam replied. It wasn't the truth, but he was bonding with Cathy and he didn't want to fuck it up.

"Josh seemed like a pretty okay guy," Sam said, trying to lighten the mood. "That kid was kind of a prick, though."

A hint of a smile finally cracked in the corner of Cathy's mouth. It didn't stick around too long though.

"Do you think I'm a bad person?" she asked.

"I think you're the kind of person who picks up strangers and takes them to medical clinics when they burst their ear drums," Sam said, a response that elicited a full smile from Cathy. "I think that's the sign of a good person, someone who gives a shit, you know?"

"Thanks for saying that, dude." Cathy said. Her shoulders lowered as she let out a long, slow breath. "I don't even know where I'm driving."

"I think we need to find a cheap motel and call it a night," Sam said. "Get up fresh tomorrow and start over."

Downtown Tallahassee glowed in the distance. A million shining beacons called out to Cathy, drawing her in. "I want to sing," she said, out of nowhere. "I feel like singing."

Sam pondered the idea of a night out on the town in Tallahassee. The introvert inside of him wanted no part of it. He craved vending machine food, a warm bed with cold, scratchy sheets, and blackout curtains. But this new side of him—the side that Cathy brought out—came to the conclusion that life is short, and if you're lucky, you only visit Tallahassee once, and those downtown lanterns sure were twinkling. Sam's hunger suddenly returned.

"Can we at least drive through somewhere first?" he asked.

#

Sam and Cathy ended up downtown where college kids got drunk during the school year. It was summer now, and the streets were sparse save for a few townies and students who lived locally. Sam was damn near in a food coma thanks to eating two burritos from a place called Taco Pete's. He trailed behind Cathy, who lugged his guitar down a neon-lit sidewalk in search of a bar with an open mic.

They soon stumbled upon a hole in the wall called Black Charlie's, which Sam thought sounded like an authentic blues bar straight out of Memphis. Upon entering, Sam realized the blackest thing about this place was the paint on the walls. White people, everywhere. An expansive, well-stocked bar took up the right side of the joint. In the middle sat four pool tables, all of which were currently in use. Flat screen TV's displayed sports everywhere you looked. But way in the back, almost an afterthought, was a small wooden stage flanked by neon beer signs. In front of the stage, two metal folding chairs held on for dear life beneath two morbidly obese women. A young white man wearing a cutoff t-shirt, a backwards baseball hat, and a blood orange spray tan occupied the stage with an acoustic guitar. He strummed and sang his best rendition of Dave Matthews' "Crash," which actually didn't sound much worse than the original. The two ladies in the folding chairs waved their arms and sang along drunkenly.

Sam spied the room to get a feel for the place while Cathy scooted past him and headed for the bar. "You want anything?" she asked.

"Just get me whatever you get," he replied, immediately regretting the power he had given her. They were both already two margaritas in, and it didn't take Cathy any time at all to flag down a bartender and order her chosen drink – bourbon mixed with Sprite. She asked the bartender about the open mic, and he pointed to a back corner of the bar where a yellow notepad sat on a sad, lonely card table.

Cathy returned to Sam and handed him the drink.

"What is this?" he asked.

"Drink it," she said. "You'll like it."

"It's clear. I prefer a brownish tint."

"Shut up," she fired back, not taking any shit. Sam smiled and wisely took a sip before following Cathy to the open mic sign-up sheet in the far corner. The lonely piece of paper contained just two names: Luke Money and Tasha Simmons. Cathy printed hers below Tasha's, then turned around just in time to catch the end of the Dave Matthews debacle. The only applause came from the two giants in the folding chairs, who screamed and demanded an encore.

"Thank you," the crooner shouted over the heads of the women, despite the fact that no one else was paying attention. "I'm Luke Money," he said, bolting from the stage with his two biggest fans in tow. Up next, a tiny African-American woman named Tasha took the stage with no introduction and no audible response from the crowd. Cathy realized that not only was no one listening, no one was even running this show. In the spirit of solidarity, Cathy clapped loudly and whistled as Tasha approached the microphone.

"Hey, thanks," Tasha said before finger picking the acoustic intro to Tracy Chapman's "Fast Car."

"Christ, this song always makes me cry," Cathy said.

Sam stood with his arms folded as Tasha began to sing. Damn. She had a good voice. A really good one. And not a soul besides the two of them was paying attention. By the time the second verse began, Sam watched Cathy retreat into the women's room, leaving him the only person alive listening to Tasha's heartbreaking cover of a bleak eighties pop classic. The song ended with a final strum and Sam applauded, attempting a whistle of his own but shooting blanks instead.

"Thanks again," Tasha whispered softly into the microphone before slipping off the stage. Sam looked around for Cathy, but she was nowhere in sight. He wandered over to the ladies' room door, where a waitress in a black cut-off midriff streamed out in a hurry.

"Excuse me," Sam said, "was there another woman in there? A blonde with a guitar?"

The waitress nodded. "I think she's just got some nerves." The waitress went back to work and Sam pushed the door open slightly.

"Hey, it's me… It's Sam," he called out. "You don't have to do this. This place sucks. Let's just get out of here."

A minute later, Cathy burst out of the restroom with her guitar strapped on, ready to do business. She strutted down the hall toward the stage, clonked up two small stairs and peered out at the bar. As she approached the mic, it squawked and sent painful feedback through the P.A. speakers. Everyone was listening now—they had no choice. Cathy lowered the microphone, tuned her guitar and allowed her lips to skirt the microphone once again.

"This is my first time doing anything like this," she confessed, startled by the sound of her amplified voice. She held her hand in a salute position above her eyebrows and squinted to find Sam in the bar. He was actually seated right in front of her in one of the metal folding chairs. He gazed up at her, an angelic silhouette blasted with floodlights from behind.

"This is a song I wrote called 'Dove,' Cathy said, pulling a guitar pick from the headstock. "This is my friend Sam's guitar. It's a beautiful guitar. Thank you Sam, wherever you are... you better still be here." With that, Cathy closed her eyes, placed her left hand into the C chord position and hovered her right hand above the strings. An eternity passed. Sam waited. At the bar, the waitress from the bathroom scoped the stage. A couple of drunks at the pool table even stopped to see what was going to happen to this beautiful drifter in the spotlight.

Cathy appeared to be holding her breath. Sam could read the tension on her face as her eyes grew wide. She was a deer in headlights. An eternity passed until she finally released all of the air bottled up in her lungs. "I'm sorry," she said, fleeing the stage with her guitar still strapped on. She brushed past Sam without even seeing him, past the pool tables, past the bar, through the front door and into the Tallahassee night.

"Shit," Sam sputtered. He gave chase, catching up with her at the end of the block waiting for a pedestrian traffic signal to change from "Don't Walk" to "Walk."

"Hey, are you okay?"

Cathy kept her gaze toward the street, avoiding eye contact. "I just need to go this way," she said. Sam instinctively hooked his right arm into hers. She peered at him, suddenly a prisoner linked to him, but a captive who made no effort to escape. Together they stood, arms snaked, until the traffic light changed.

#

Cathy didn't say much as she and Sam watched the lights of downtown disappear into the rear view mirror as the Monte Carlo took to the outskirts of Tallahassee. Almost instinctively, Cathy pulled into a Super 8 Motel adjacent to a convenience store.

"Let me pay," Sam insisted as Cathy unbuckled her seat belt.

"I got it," she replied. Sam pulled out forty dollars from his pocket anyway. "Please. I want to." Cathy hesitated, then took the cash and stuck it into her bra.

#

With two beeps and a click, the door labeled 218 opened and a pitch black room lit up in the orange glow of incandescent wall sconces. Inside, a pair of full-sized beds with green quilted comforters greeted them below Santa Fe inspired oil paintings signed "Donald '96."

"I'll take that one," Cathy said, indicating the bed on the inner part of the room. "Those fucking air conditioners get too

157

cold." The weighted door swung closed with a loud click behind Sam. He glanced back toward it.

"I think I'm going to walk down to that store," Sam said. "Do you want anything?"

"Maybe some water," Cathy replied.

Twenty minutes later Sam returned with a twenty-ounce bottle of water, a two-liter bottle of Sprite, and a large bottle of cheap bourbon. "They didn't have any good stuff," he grumbled. Cathy's hair was still wet from taking a shower, and the bra that previously lived underneath her blouse was suddenly nowhere to be found. Cathy eyed the bottles and then Sam. "What are you waiting for?"

#

Half the bourbon was gone, and so were Sam and Cathy. Cathy leaned against her headboard with her eyes peeled at a decrepit motel TV that filled the darkened room with flashes and flickers. Sam laid down flat on the bed, mostly drunk, glaring up at a water stain on the ceiling.

"I'll bet this place has asbestos," he said.

"What's asbestos?" Cathy responded, and the room fell silent for another two minutes as a local news anchor flubbed the nightly telecast.

"Where to tomorrow?" Sam asked, breaking through the iron curtain.

"The fuck out of Florida," Cathy quipped.

Sam swore the water stains were growing and bulging before his eyes. "So, what happened to you up there? Did you forget the words?"

Cathy continued to stare at the TV. "No, I knew the words," she responded. "I couldn't find you."

Sam sat up, his head a helicopter, and through the eighty proof blur he spied his guitar case perched at the foot of Cathy's bed. He stared at it for a good long while, until Cathy finally caught him.

"Why are you staring at the guitar?" Cathy slurred.

"Because I want you to play it," Sam pressed.

"Don't ask me that. I don't play when I've been drinking... this much." Sam's eyes locked onto hers, refusing to take no for an answer.

"You want me to play it?" she asked. Sam nodded in noiseless anticipation.

"Fine," she said. "But don't look at me while I'm singing."

"Seriously?" he asked.

"Yes. I mean it."

Sam complied by lying back on the bed, his gaze once again landing on the ceiling above. Cathy took a long swig from the bourbon on the night stand next to her. She slung the guitar

over her shoulder, sat back down on the bed and began to fin-
gerpick a delicate, folksy rhythm. And then her mouth opened.

My dove, you come to me

and sleep in my passenger seat

little wings, white like winter, you wake and fly

into a blue sky turning green

colors we can change to anything

when our hands and our hearts are on fire

Sam closed his eyes and listened to every word.

I don't know what I'm supposed to say

Some words just get in the way

When I feel this alone

I wanna take you home

If I asked you to sing 'I'd Have To Be Crazy'

would you crumble, crying all the while

Last night I had a dream

You and I and nothing in between

and the stars shined like diamonds in the sky

But I don't know what I'm supposed to say

My words just get in the way

When I feel this alone

I wanna take you home

Cathy fingerpicked an intricate instrumental section and
then stopped abruptly.

"I don't have a third verse for that one yet," she said, breaking the spell. Sam's eyes opened and he sat up, speechless. Cathy slid the guitar off, gazed at Sam and patted a spot on the bed next to her. Sam blinked with weighted eyes, the cheap alcohol fueling his bravery. He climbed off his bed and found his way to Cathy's side of the room. He chose a spot next to her on the lumpy mattress, and together they sat and stared quietly at the window-mounted air conditioner as it hummed and spit out the occasional icicle. The vibration of the humming unit filled the room with a unique soundtrack—a buzzing heartbeat. Sam lifted his hand above the bed and let it hover above Cathy's, finally finding the nerve to drop it on top of hers. Her face turned toward his, a playful stare that lasted so long that they finally broke out in laughter—teenagers again. Sam's face angled toward the carpet momentarily until Cathy took control and turned his face back toward hers.

"Put your face close to my face," Cathy muttered, the bourbon still fresh on her tongue. Sam leaned in slowly until the space between their noses measured in millimeters. The pair wavered and floated endlessly until the gap finally closed and their lips engaged. Faintly, carelessly, underneath a tacky painting from the nineties featuring a crested butte, Cathy and Sam shared their first kiss. A shockwave rolled through Sam. Cathy's nerves tingled. When the kiss ended, Cathy's eyes danced back

161

and forth trying to decide which of Sam's pupils she wanted to focus on. She nodded and smiled sheepishly, then shook her head no. She repeated the performance while Sam laughed and mocked her, then kissed her again, so soft and so sweet.

"Can I ask you something?" Sam asked. Cathy blinked playfully, her eyes heavy, the bourbon doing its job. "Okay. Ask me."

"Was Ollie sick, I mean, before he …"

Cathy's flushed face suddenly turned lighter, colder, like a rabbit in winter. She studied Sam's face. The ripples in the water began to multiply as Sam realized what he had done.

"I'm sorry," Sam said. "I don't know why I asked that."

Cathy let go of a long, deep, alcohol-tinged breath. "I'm going to sleep now," she said. Sam closed his eyes tightly as Cathy slid off the bed and escaped to the other one. Cathy clicked off the wall sconce, filling half the room with darkness, before burying her head beneath a mountain of pillows. Sam sat and stared at the remaining wall sconce for two minutes, fixating on a tiny sticker that read "Made in China." Sam finally stood up and turned off the light, collapsing onto his bed.

CHAPTER 15

Sam woke at seven-thirty sharp as the morning sun penetrated the blackout curtains, searing a line of UV rays into the right side of his face. He had a pounding headache, thanks to last night's drink of choice, and his bladder begged for mercy. Sam sat up and quickly discovered that Cathy's side of the bed was empty. Concerned, he angled toward the bathroom and found it equally barren.

"Fuck me," Sam mumbled. He quickly emptied his bladder. As the intoxicants drained from his body, a million scenarios raced through Sam's head, and he settled on the one where Cathy was simply gone. Sam finished the world's longest pee and raced to the window, whipping open the curtains and filling the room with undiluted, brazen sunlight. As his pupils dilated,

163

his eyes found the parking lot. The Monte Carlo remained, poorly-parked, just where they had left it the night before.

Sam released a sigh of relief, but the mystery remained. Cathy was still gone. Sam considered getting dressed and searching the convenience store or the Denny's attached to it. Maybe she had gone there. But he didn't want to miss her in passing, so he stayed where he was, sweating bullets. He turned back to his bed to discover that her bag remained, as did her tattered chipboard guitar case.

An hour passed. Sam took a shower and forced himself to get dressed. He turned on the TV but couldn't pay attention to it. He glared out the motel window again but saw no sign of Cathy. He turned back toward the room, and that's when he spotted something strange on her guitar case. There was a piece of paper sticking out where the top lid met the bottom. Sam moved in for a closer inspection and discovered that the paper was actually a $100 bill. Ben Franklin's folded face beamed back at him, begging to be released from the bear trap he was caught in.

Just as Sam kneeled down to satisfy his curiosity, the motel door opened. Sam flung around to find Cathy standing with two large Styrofoam food containers and a pair of coffees gripped against her chest.

"Do you like eggs?" she asked.

"I'm allergic," Sam replied.

Cathy's face turned sour. *Seriously?*

"Well, there's bacon," she responded, handing Sam an over-stuffed box of grease. Sam took one last look at Benjamin Franklin before abandoning his investigation.

#

Sam and Cathy hit the road much later than planned, but Sam was quickly adapting to Cathy's preferred method of fly-ing—by the seat of her pants. Her random nature flew com-pletely in the face of his preferred routines, but every time he witnessed the highway's wind turn her hair into a tempest at seventy miles per hour there wasn't much else in the world to care about.

Traffic moving west on Interstate 10 was mercifully light. Less than an hour after the day's journey had begun, the Monte Carlo whipped past the metal sign in the median that read "Now leaving Florida." At the moment of exodus, Sam considered all the things he was leaving behind. His house and his banana tree. A 400-acre field full of granite tombstones that he had personal-ly etched, and the sinkhole that had forced him to finally make a move. The last eight years of his life. Sam twisted back and glared out the windshield at the already-burning Florida sun, then turned back around to see endless layers of cirrus clouds unfolding along the Alabama skyline. Sam nodded silently. Bring on the clouds.

There was no talk of last night's romance, not even a whiff of it, and by the time Sam and Cathy reached the bustling town of Mobile, Sam had passed out in the passenger seat with his mouth hanging open. Cathy pushed ahead down the billboard-lined interstate, making note of a series of advertisements for DeSoto National Forest, a "lush, piney woods retreat with silky streams and plenty of restrooms." The billboard directed her to "exit Highway 98 North," and she was a little more than intrigued. She glared at Sam, still unconscious.

"Sam … hey, do you want to check out that park?" she asked at normal volume. Sam didn't stir an inch.

Cathy pressed on—"If you don't want to go, say something now. Say something now, goddammit." Sam stirred slightly but didn't wake up.

Cathy grinned.

Half an hour later, Sam woke up and stretched his impossibly long arms. He peered out the windshield at a new landscape. Things looked… different. Six lanes of the interstate had shrunken to four. Billboards and buildings were few and far between.

"Where are we?" he asked.

"Detour," Cathy said with a grin. "I saw a sign for a national preserve. Thought it might be relaxing." Soon the road had narrowed from four lanes to two and the claustrophobic Sam began to feel as though the world was closing in on him. Cathy could feel the tension in the car as the Monte Carlo wound around steep cliff turns.

"My God, would you look at these mountains," Cathy piped. "No wonder John Denver wrote such good fucking songs."

Sam's face wrinkled as he glared out at the lifting rock formations that blurred by. "This isn't … we're not … this isn't Colorado, is it?"

It damn well could've been for all he knew. The car sputtered and rolled through majestic gray and white mountains with jagged cliffs and smooth, silvery landings. Pine Savannahs, Flatwoods, and Longleaf Pines stood tall and skinny—reaching a mile into the sky—overlooking the park from their vertical vantage points. The lush forestry stretched out to the horizon until the treetops became dobs of acrylic paint—a Bob Ross painting come to life.

"John Denver sucked, by the way," Sam added.

A sign up ahead pointed the way to "Black Creek Wilderness."

"That's where we're going," Cathy declared, and by now, Sam was little more than a hostage to her whims.

"Go wherever you want," he said. His only other choice was to dive out of the car as it drove over the dusty, rugged terrain at twenty-five miles per hour. He placed his odds of surviving such an attempt at four-to-one, depending on whether or not his head hit any rocks on the way out.

The Monte Carlo entered Black Creek Wilderness and began to drive alongside a beautiful, caramel-tinted stream flanked by pine trees that led to a tiered waterfall. "It looks just like the billboard," Cathy opined, pulling the car to a stop on the side of the road. She killed the engine and allowed the sounds of nature to fill the car.

"Would you listen to that?" Cathy asked. "Just… listen."

Sam indulged her, feigning interest. "What are we listening to?" he asked.

Cathy took Sam's hand and squeezed it. "Silence," she said. "Fucking silence."

Cathy climbed out of the car and strutted over to the edge of the road overlooking the river. Sam stayed in the car and thought about going back to sleep, but didn't. It was too quiet to sleep. The only audible noise was the flicker of water lapping over and under rocks, and the occasional bird.

"I need to pee, I think," Sam said to himself.

He got out of the Monte Carlo on the passenger side, catching Cathy's glance as he shuffled off into some nearby bushes. He picked a pine tree, turned away from the car and let nature take its course. Cathy turned around. "I can see you peeing," she said. A startled Sam jerked and accidentally peed on his shoe.

"These trees aren't big enough to hide behind!" he yelled. Cathy laughed loudly.

It didn't take long for the wilderness to win Sam over. He and Cathy sat on a flat rock at the edge of the watercourse with their legs dangled over the side. The length disparity between Cathy's mid-range gams and Sam's daddy long legs was almost comical.

"I bet if you stretched you could dip your toe in," Cathy said.

"Probably, but I'm not risking it," Sam replied. "I can't swim."

"First you don't drive and now you don't swim. I'm starting to think you're making it up as you go."

"I'm serious."

"How did you never learn how to swim?"

"I had chronic ear infections when I was a baby. Had to have these tubes put in. The left ear drum ended up with a big hole that never healed. I can't get water in it."

169

"You don't have much luck with your ears, huh?" Cathy inquired.

"Never have."

Sam shook his head and stared at the waterfall and the trees that stretched as far as the eye could see.

"This is like a Thomas Kinkade painting," Sam trilled with a straight face. Cathy flashed him an odd look. Sam felt a suction noise flow through his right ear followed by a loud pop. And just like that, the sounds of nature doubled. He touched his right ear like it was a foreign object. For a moment, everything just seemed so loud.

"Are you okay?" Cathy asked.

"I can hear out of my right ear again," Sam said, rubbing the inside of it with his index finger. "It's so weird. I had forgotten what it's like to hear out of the right side of my head."

"Nature healed you," Cathy said with a smile. Sam stood up and stretched, then glanced back at the Monte Carlo in the distance. His bonsai tree sat on top of the car, getting some much-needed sunlight.

"I wish I had a camera," Sam said, before returning to the rock and sitting back down next to Cathy. He sat deliberately closer than before, allowing his leg to touch hers. The contact wasn't lost on her as she gazed out on the water.

"Ollie would've liked it here," Cathy mused. Sam examined her with sympathetic eyes, surprised by her sudden openness. He chose his next words more carefully than he had the night before in the motel.

"What was he like?" Sam asked.

"He was into everything," Cathy said. "He was the most in-quisitive kid I ever met. He loved to learn, and he never met a stranger. God knows where he got his social skills, certainly not from me or his father."

"Rich? That guy with the binoculars. Was he...?"

Cathy shook her head strongly. "No. Rich was a later addi-tion. Ollie never knew his father... and he was better for it." Cathy's eyes found a leaf caught in the unstoppable current be-ing carried to its unknown destination. She closed her eyes as the wind whistled by. It was as if Ollie himself was pulsing through those sun-kissed pines.

"You know—he was just learning how to be a kid," she said. "He just turned two. He'd run up to me, just blathering. I wouldn't understand a single thing he was saying, but damn if he wasn't communicating. He'd get so mad at me when I didn't know the words he was trying to say. He'd just look at me with those big green eyes. They'd just destroy me."

"I'm so sorry," Sam said. "Whatever happened. That kind of loss, it's..."

171

"It was an accident," Cathy declared. "A terrible, terrible accident." Cathy stared into the unknown until her gaze finally broke and found Sam. He could feel her pressured gaze saying, *Your turn buddy, I just showed you part of my soul, what does yours look like?* He scratched his chin and found himself lost in the same current.

"I have a scar on my chin, under my beard" Sam said, his head angled upwards. "From here to here." He drew a curved line from the right side of his face down under his chin and then over another inch or so. "Car accident."

"So that's why you don't drive," Cathy guessed. Sam offered a half smile, then took her hand in his without asking. He traced his finger softly around the top of it, moving between her knuckles and up to her fingertips then tracing the edges around to her palm. "What are you doing?" she asked.

"I like your hands," Sam said. He interlocked his fingers with hers, and together they watched the caramel-colored Black Creek waters churn west with determination toward the Pacific Ocean.

They stayed in the park long enough to watch the sun sink low in the western sky. The road calling, they then drove northwest into an orange sky, past endless pine trees that eventually thinned as the horizon turned black. The winding two-lane road offered no artificial illumination to guide them in their quest, so

Cathy utilized the Monte Carlo's bright headlamps to keep the road ahead visible. Every few miles, a car would appear on the horizon and Cathy would dip the lights back to their normal setting, which lit up a scant thirty feet at best. If a deer were standing in the road, it would be a goner, and so would Cathy's car. They saw a few of them, scampering near the tree line. As luck would have it, the deer chose to stay near the safety of the trees on this particular night.

After miles of pitch black countryside, Sam and Cathy finally spotted a sign in the distance that read "Welcome to Havensburg, Mississippi. Stay awhile."

"I think they want us to stay awhile," Cathy joked.

The road widened, street lights appeared, and a city emerged. They drove past a Wal-Mart, a forgotten mall and a community college that had fallen asleep for the summer. They wound through an old neighborhood lined with one hundred-year-old oak trees guarding one hundred-year-old frame houses. They crossed two sets of train tracks before they found themselves in a deserted downtown district where the only visible signs of life appeared to be coming from a cedar barn with a metal roof situated next to yet another set of train tracks. Howl's Depot was an old saw mill that had been repurposed as a honky tonk, and Cathy's eyes lit up as soon as she saw it.

"That looks like fun," she said, gleaming. Sam was unimpressed by the squadron of oversized pickups that filled the dirt parking lot, and his legs were aching, but he couldn't deny the excitement in Cathy's eyes as she rolled the window down and heard a Hank Williams song blasting from the place.

"You wanna go in there, don't you?" Sam asked skeptically.

"Hell, yeah. Why not?"

"You sure you don't wanna just get some food, find a motel, call it a night?"

Cathy glared at him, on to his game. "You need to stretch those long legs of yours," she insisted. Sam just shook his head as Cathy squeezed the Monte Carlo between two giant Dodge Ram trucks and killed the engine.

"Come on," she said. "I owe you a drink."

#

The scene on the outside paled in comparison to the glorious, beer-soaked havoc inside. Sam and Cathy pushed through the heavy, ten-foot-tall wooden doors and discovered the place absolutely packed with locals, young and old, in cowboy and cowgirl attire. The room was brightly lit by ancient phosphorescent work lights that radiated above a creaky hardwood floor covered in sawdust. Busy bars flanked both sides of the large dance floor, and a full band played classic country & western swing from an elevated stage.

"This is my kind of place!" Cathy exclaimed. In their casual,
non-country attire, they were clearly out of their element. Sam,
in particular, stuck out like a sore thumb, but his pearl snap shirt
did give him a tiny amount of street cred amongst the rednecks.

"I'm going to get us some tequila shots," Cathy declared.

"Please don't get tequila shots," Sam tried to say, but it was
too late—Cathy had already disappeared into the bar area. Sam
could see that this was her element, and he did his best to adapt.
He leaned against a wooden railing and scanned the venue—a
mini-Urban Cowboy without the mechanical bull. His eyes
eventually landed on the crowded dance floor, where a throng
of two-steppers and spinners whipped, stomped and dosey-
doed. Cathy soon returned with the promised shots, giving one
to Sam.

"I splurged on Patrón," she said. She held up the shot glass.
"To new places," she said, clinking Sam's glass. They downed
the shots simultaneously, Sam wincing a little harder than Cathy.
Cathy slipped the shot glass from Sam's fingers and placed both
of them down on the railing. She eyed the dance floor. "Let's go
dance," she declared.

"No, I can't. I don't." Sam said. "You go ahead."

"You don't drive. You don't swim. Now you don't dance.
Are you kidding me? I can't two-step alone," Cathy pleaded. She
squeezed his hand tight.

"Really, I don't dance. Please. I'll watch from here."

Cathy shook her head. She didn't just want to dance, she wanted to dance with Sam. "You better not take your eyes off me," she said.

"I won't," Sam vowed, and he meant it. Cathy rushed to the dance floor, guns-a-blazin'. Sam watched from the bullpen like a pitcher with a weak fastball. It didn't take long until Cathy found a partner, a tall cowboy with a neatly trimmed goatee and a belt buckle the size of Texas—also coincidentally in the shape of Texas.

The band played an up-tempo fiddle instrumental and the cowboy had his way with Cathy, spinning and dipping her like a man who did this routinely. The guy was good. Sam watched, not really jealous, but feeling slightly inferior. Cathy was clearly having a blast. Sam smiled. She needed this. The song reached a crescendo, then ended in a furious twang. The cowboy dipped Cathy again, and then the pair came up for a breath of air.

"Where did you come from?" the cowboy asked, his hand touching Cathy's lower back. Cathy smiled. "Florida," she replied.

The band's lead singer strapped on an acoustic guitar and approached the microphone. "We're gonna slow it down a little bit for you two-steppers out there," he said, as the band kicked into a slow waltz. "This is as an old slow-dancing song. It's about being on the road when the road is all you have."

The cowboy pulled Cathy close at her waist and slid his hand down her right arm until his fingers locked into hers. Tequila on her breath, whiskey on his, they began an intimate two-step. Sam watched, growing more uneasy as the song continued.

"Where you stayin' tonight?" the cowboy whispered into Cathy's ear as their dance intensified. She could feel his eyes and hands all over her. Before she could answer, a foreign body slid between them. It was Sam.

"Excuse me," Sam interrupted. "I believe this dance is mine."

"The fuck are you?" the cowboy asked, his posture defensive. The trio stood motionless as the wave of dancers circled around them. Sam and Cathy were suddenly the eye of a hurricane.

"This is my friend," Cathy declared. The cowboy laughed as he backed away.

"Be my guest, asshole," the cowboy said before storming off the dance floor. Sam heard the remark, but didn't care. He pulled Cathy close, pressed his cheek to hers and did his best not to step on her toes as the band kicked into the chorus.

Sam's feet were all over the place. Cathy leaned into Sam's left ear and spoke as loudly as she could. "Follow my lead. One and two and one … one and two and one." Sam looked down, using Cathy's feet as his vanguard. He finally got the hang of it, at least to the point where he was only hobbling Cathy's ankle once a minute. He glanced back up to see Cathy's howling green eyes alive with light that shined directly through him. She lifted her arms up and wrapped her wrists around his neck, pulling him close. "Where have you been all my life, Sam Stone?" she asked.

Sam grinned, and together they danced to the last chorus. That's when Sam kissed Cathy right there on that dance floor. Soft and deep, their tongues dipping and glancing like prize fighters. Sam opened his eyes slightly to find Cathy's closed tightly, the kiss lingering. In that moment, nothing else mattered.

Hand in hand, Sam and Cathy said goodbye to the honky tonk with the big metal roof and dashed into the parking lot toward the car. Their path guided them along train tracks where Cathy, three tequilas in now, let loose of Sam's grip and tiptoed along the iron rails, doing her best balancing act.

"Be careful!" Sam hollered. Cathy laughed, let out a "woo!" and then lost her balance, slipping off the rail toward the gravel below. She didn't fall hard enough to lose her footing, but the cowboy caught her by the elbow anyway.

"Well, look who it is," he muttered, his bottom lip packed with snuff. Cathy aggressively pulled away from his grip. "I'm fine" she said. "Thank you."

Sam caught up from behind as the cowboy took Cathy by the arm again.

"Why don't you come on home with me tonight?" the cowboy pleaded, drunk and bulletproof.

"Hey—let go of my arm, you fucking asshole," Cathy said.

"Let go of her arm," Sam said firmly. He inched closer and could see a buck knife looped into the cowboy's belt.

"You had your dance, hippie," the cowboy slurred. "This whore's goin' with me."

"I don't think so," Sam said. Cathy tore away from the cowboy's grip as Sam rushed forward. The cowboy reached for his knife but it slipped to the ground. He took a swing at Sam— a real haymaker—but Sam ducked and it missed him by a country mile. Sam returned the favor, connecting with a whopping right to the big man's jaw. Skoal spewed from the cowboy's lips as his legs turned to jelly. He fell back toward the train tracks, his forehead whacking against the iron rail as his body slammed to the ground. The rail had opened a five-inch gash in his forehead. Blood spilled out at a rapid pace, turning the speckled white and grey gravel a dark crimson.

"Shit," Sam panicked.

"Let's get outta here," Cathy said.

"No. We can't leave him here. He'll bleed to death."

"He was going to fuckin' rape me!"

"Go to the car and look in the zipper pocket on my sleeping bag. There's a first aid kit."

"What?"

"Please, go get it!"

"Sam—we have to leave!"

"Cathy—please!"

A dazed Cathy limped toward the car while Sam tore off his shirt and fashioned a homemade tourniquet around the cowboy's gushing head. The burgundy plasma quickly soaked through the light blue denim, forcing Sam to tighten the bandage.

"You son of a bitch. This is my favorite shirt."

Cathy returned with the first aid kit. Sam snatched it and quickly went to work. He pulled out a mini bottle of alcohol, twisted the top off, and poured a good amount onto the wound through the work shirt. The cowboy's eyes popped open, and he began to struggle. Sam pinned his arms down with his knees. "Hold your ass still," he asserted. The cowboy was too in shock to fight, so he just lay there, mumbling incoherently.

Satisfied that the tourniquet had done its job, Sam pulled out a plastic case that contained needles and sewing thread.

"Hold down his arms," he commanded Cathy. "He's not going to like this at all."

"What are you going to do with that?" Cathy asked.

"Please, just do it."

Cathy did the best she could to pin the cowboy's arms down. She watched in disbelief as Sam threaded a needle in the black of night with three tequilas in his system, then masterfully began to stitch up the cowboy's forehead. As the first needle prick entered his forehead he kicked as though he had been lit on fire.

"Lay still, you dumb mother fucker!" Sam, said as he dug his knee further into the cowboy's shoulder.

Cathy couldn't believe what she was seeing. "Where did you learn how to do this?" she asked. Sam didn't answer, he just kept stitching. When the deed was done, Sam stood up, shirt-less, his stomach, chest and jeans covered in the stranger's blood. He took a step back as the cowboy sat up in a daze, found his feet, and stumbled into the dark parking lot without saying another word. Cathy glared at Sam as the light of a freight train neared. The engine roared by and Sam watched his shirt-turned-tourniquet get ripped to shreds underneath the force of the train's chugging wheels. As the train let out a deafening whistle, Sam took Cathy by the hand and led her back to the car.

CHAPTER 16

Alan couldn't see or hear anything for his first few seconds of consciousness, but he could feel something loose hanging from his chin. He pried open his powder-stung eyes and discovered that not only was his head buried in an ejected airbag, but that the foreign object hanging from his chin was actually his chin itself. The canvas ridges of the airbag had sliced the skin clean off on impact—an impact he couldn't even remember. Alan touched the bottom of his face and immediately winced in pain. He lifted his hand in front of his eyes. Though his vision was blurry, there was no mistaking the sight of blood on his fingers.

A terrifying female scream wailed outside of the car. Somehow, Alan found the strength to move his neck enough to peer through the driver's side window. He was not on the road and he was not anywhere near it. He was in someone's yard, and that someone was a woman in her thirties in a blue t-shirt and jean shorts standing in the grass with no shoes on. Alan coughed violently, sending a spray of bloody saliva onto the deflated air bag as the screams continued. Alan didn't know if the woman was wailing at him or someone else. Her cries seemed to be focused on something in front of the car. Alan tried with all his might, but could not see around the airbag or through the cracked windshield. He could barely move at all, and he felt himself slipping away. He lost consciousness, and when he woke a firefighter was toiling to free him from the wrecked BMW. Alan twisted in pain as the fireman, whose name plate read "Hoffman," cut loose his tightly bound seat belt.

"Hey buddy, hold still, okay?" Hoffman insisted. "You could have a broken neck."

"I don't think anything's broken," a delirious Alan said. "Why was that woman screaming?"

He couldn't hear the screams anymore. They had turned to sobs.

"Please hold still."

The firefighter wrapped a plastic neck brace around Alan's head. In his peripheral vision, Alan spotted two ambulances parked outside the passenger window, their lights ablaze.

"Why are there two ambulances?" Alan asked in a panic. Hoffman didn't answer. Alan drifted again as the memories of his day came flooding back; his marathon shift at the hospital, the surgery he had somehow completed, the beginning of his drive home.

"Did I fall asleep? What the hell happened?"

An EMT joined the firefighter, entering the car from the passenger side. He tended to Alan's chin, cleaning the wound and wrapping his face with gauze.

"Hang in there, fella, you're going to be okay," the EMT said.

"Did I hit something?" Alan asked. The EMT and the firefighter made eye contact but neither spoke.

"Will someone please fucking tell me what happened?" Alan screamed, on the verge of tears.

"Hang tight, man," Hoffman said. "We'll be right back."

Alan found himself alone in the car, unable to move. The neck brace forced him to stare straight ahead. The powder from the air bags had finally settled, and through the kaleidoscope of cracks in the windshield he could see the EMTs kneeling down in front of the car. Alan's face flooded with tears as he sat immobile for the longest six minutes of his life. To make matters worse, the woman's sobs were now accompanied by a man's outbursts as well.

Hoffman and the EMT finally returned to Alan, pushing a rolling metal stretcher toward the back of the car.

"We're going to get you out of here real slow now, okay?" Hoffman said. Alan closed his eyes tight as they peeled him out of his seat.

"FUCK!" Howling pain wailed through every nerve in Alan's body. He feared his neck was indeed broken. The EMT and firefighter carried him toward the rear of the car where the stretcher waited. Alan attempted to turn around, but the neck brace prevented it.

"Let me down," Alan cried. Somehow his legs wriggled loose from the grip of the emergency responders. His feet hit the ground, miraculously holding the weight of his body as he twisted back toward the accident, unbelievable agony shooting through every limb.

"Hey, get back here!" the EMT yelled. Alan limped three feet before Hoffman and the EMT caught him. The pair forcefully carried him back to the stretcher and strapped him down.

"I'm a fucking doctor," Alan said, but his cries fell on deaf ears. The EMT strapped Alan's arms down to his sides and wheeled him toward the ambulance in the driveway. Alan could see a crowd forming along the neighbor's fence line. Onlookers. Gawkers. Looky-loos. The pictures on their faces registered shock, dismay, and terror. The EMT pulled open the back of the ambulance doors and prepared to lift the stretcher inside, a move that required him to spin the stretcher around 180 degrees. This four-second window was the only glimpse Alan would ever get of the accident scene. There, twenty yards away, on a manicured lawn in front of a dented BMW, lay the lifeless bodies of two young boys. A pair of EMTs worked desperately to administer CPR, their sweaty, gripped palms repetitively collapsing the boys' chests with desperate force. Alan screamed as the metal legs of the stretcher collapsed and jolted him into the ambulance. Alan's cries were muffled when the EMT closed the doors, got in the driver's seat, and drove Alan back to the hospital he had left less than an hour ago.

CHAPTER 17

The Monte Carlo plodded through the heart of the Bible Belt on a muggy Mississippi morning, its jumpy speedometer rarely clocking above 60 mph. After stopping in the middling town of Jackson for a quick mid-morning breakfast, Sam and Cathy set their sights westbound once again, their impromptu detour complete, for now.

They didn't speak much of the night before, or their bizarre encounter along the train tracks. It was all something of a blur, anyway. After leaving the honky-tonk, they had trucked back to the interstate and settled on the cheapest motel they could find. Earlier in the evening, as they danced on that sawdust-covered dance floor, made of one hundred-year-old Mississippi pine, Cathy had every intention of making love to Sam later in the evening. But the pair had ended up crashing on separate beds in the motel. It was for the best. As a rule of thumb, it's rarely a good idea to make love whilst covered in a stranger's blood.

Mississippi flew by, and the tiny town of Tallulah welcomed them to Louisiana with little fanfare. Blink-and-you-miss-them dots on the map like Delhi and Rayville didn't offer much more in the way of scenery as the drive entered its fifth hour. Sam noticed that the interstate seemed to run just far enough away from these tiny towns to get much of a peek at anything. It was as if the little town of Arcadia, Louisiana didn't want anything to do with your fancy motor car, thank you very much. "Stay away from Locust Street, Asshole Tourists" the sign would read, if such a sign existed.

Sam understood the feeling, and he knew that Cathy did, too. They had kept people at arm's length for years to prevent anyone from getting too close for comfort—there were scary things behind those curtains. Collectively, they threatened to do the exact same thing to each other, though it was unclear if either truly realized it. But here they were together for some reason, on this journey, pulled west by an unknown entity. It was here, above the magnetic rumbling of the Louisiana interstate, that Sam felt like he might actually see the real Cathy.

Cathy glanced over and caught Sam looking. "What?"

"Nothing," he replied.

Cathy let out a long breath. "So when we get to Texas, how long are we staying?" The word "we" shot through Sam like lightning. It wasn't a word he had ever thought of when referring to them. He stared at the highway while Cathy stared at him.

"You didn't think I was going to let you stay there, did you?" Cathy asked. "You are coming to California with me, right?"

Officially on the spot, Sam froze. He finally turned toward her, still a bit dumbfounded.

"Is that what you want?" he asked.

Cathy furrowed her brow. She lit a cigarette, took a drag, and then aimed it out the window.

"That was kinda the question I was asking you, Sam," she responded, the highway wind rifling through her hair. A bug splattered against the windshield. Cathy hit the wipers to knock it off and scattered a trail of insect guts along the wiper path.

#

Sam stared out the passenger window at what seemed like the 400th casino billboard in the last sixty miles along I-20, and he glanced at Cathy and wondered if she was looking at them as well. Of course she was, there was nothing else to see on this stretch. The car had grown remarkably quiet over the last hour.

The squealing belts inside the engine had lulled Sam and Cathy into a state of reflection.

The dry, lifeless highway went on for miles, but somewhere near Minden, water suddenly surrounded them on all sides. The late afternoon sun beamed and bounced off of the glass pools like giant mirrors, but as quickly as they came, the lakes disappeared, and the road became a wasteland of billboards and trees once again. Not a moment too soon, the Monte Carlo found water again as Sam and Cathy crossed the muscular Red River from Bossier City into Shreveport.

And there they were: the fucking casinos. Half a dozen of them, flanking both sides of the river, each one advertising "Prime Rib for $4.99." Bossier and Shreveport were twin cities not unlike Minneapolis and St. Paul, Minnesota. Without snow, but with equally annoying accents.

"This is like the sad version of Las Vegas," Cathy mused.

"I thought Las Vegas was the sad version of Las Vegas," Sam retorted.

"You're thinking of Reno." Cathy drove aimlessly, passing the casinos, then doubling back. "I don't know which of these shit holes to pull into," she said.

"Who says we have to stay at a casino in the first place?" Sam asked. "There's a Travelodge right over there. Forty-nine bucks."

"Yeah, but the casinos will comp your room if you gamble," Cathy said.

"Oh, did you bring gambling money? I left my gambling money in Florida."

As night fell on northern Louisiana, Cathy pulled the Monte Carlo into the Boom City Casino & Hotel, a perfectly square, eight-story stucco nightmare designed solely to take you for every penny you dared gamble.

Sam and Cathy wandered through a packed, carpet-lined casino thick with cigarette smoke. High rollers they were not—it was more of a social experiment than anything. As they strolled past an old married couple playing video poker, Cathy found Sam's hand, stretching his fingers apart to sneak hers in-between.

"Jesus... I'm having flashbacks," Cathy said as they weaved through an endless sea of slot machines.

"Yeah, I think they give you cash here instead of craft store gift cards," Sam said slyly. Cathy laughed and shook her head.

"Did you ever?"

"I did. It's smart. Totally illegal, but smart."

Cathy stared at the diamond-shaped patterns crisscrossing the carpet. "So here's the thing," she said, leading him to a row of penny slots.

Cathy leaned in to whisper in his ear. "I have nine thousand dollars cash in this guitar case," she said. Sam's eyes grew wide as he focused on the case—the one he had seen the hundred dollar bill sticking out of.

"Where did you... ?"

"RJ's got raided the morning we left town. I was in the right place at the right time. I don't even really know how it happened."

"Wait. It's not your money?"

Cathy stuck her finger up to his lips. "It's my money now."

"But ... is someone looking for you? Like, tracking you or something? Are you in any trouble?"

Cathy shook her head. "I got paid cash there. They don't even know my full name."

"What is your full name?" Sam inquired.

"Cathy Wanda Peabody," she said, embarrassed. "It's not pretty, I know."

"It's a fine set of names," Sam responded. Her disclosure had knocked the wind out of him, but here he was—still holding her hand, butterflies swirling in his stomach like some kind of junior high student. He felt free and irresponsible at the same time, but if he had learned anything from Cathy, it was to live in the moment. After all, there are only so many moments.

#

192

"Let's put it all on black," Cathy said as the pair approached a packed roulette table.

"All of what?" Sam asked. Cathy pulled out a single $100 bill from her purse and smiled.

"Whoa," Sam said. "High roller." Cathy placed the bill in Sam's hand and closed his fist tightly around it, then nudged him toward the action. Sam squeezed between a couple of overly enthusiastic gamblers in silk Hawaiian shirts, waited for the next spin, then handed the Benjamin Franklin to the roulette dealer.

"On the table," the dealer said impatiently.

"I'm sorry?"

"You can't hand me money."

"Oh, sorry."

Embarrassed, Sam placed the money on the table, and in return received four green twenty five dollar casino chips. He glanced back at Cathy and held them up, mouthing the words *are you sure?* With a thumbs up from Cathy, Sam placed all the chips down on black. The dealer waited for all bets to be placed, scanned the table and called out, "No more bets!"

The dealer set the wheel in motion and dropped the marble into play. Sam watched it bounce around haphazardly, carrying a dozen destinies in its journey. With a click, click, clack, the marble found its final resting place.

Red. Thirty four.

Sam sunk, but Cathy didn't appear nearly as dejected. "Can't win 'em all," she declared.

On the elevator ride up to their sixth floor suite, Sam noticed Cathy appeared quiet and slightly despondent.

"Everything okay?" he asked, but before she could answer, the elevator dinged and deposited them at their floor.

#

Sam sat on a pink queen-sized bed surrounded by walls adorned with peeling, gold paper. The hotel was called Boomtown, but the boom must have happened more than a few years ago—it was bust city now. Sam stretched out on the bed and reached for the remote control on the adjacent night stand, only to find it glued in place.

"Are you fucking kidding me?"

Sam managed to press enough buttons to get the damn thing to turn on, at least. The TV played nothing but static on every channel, and Sam couldn't get it to turn off. Oh well, fuck it, he thought. Background noise. Sam looked up toward the bathroom. The shower had been running for almost half an hour now. Sam glanced at the phone on the nightstand that sat atop a Gideon's bible. He picked up the receiver, pressed nine, and dialed a number. He waited, fully expecting to get an answering machine, but after eight rings, someone picked up.

"Hello?" the voice on the other end muttered. It was a man's voice with a thick Hispanic accent, someone completely foreign to Sam.

"Who is this?" Sam asked sharply.

"Uh—who is this?"

"Is Gary there?"

"Gary? No. He left already. He went to the horses."

"Horses?"

"Sam Houston. The races. Who is this?"

"How do you know Gary?"

"I have to go now, I think."

"Wait—"

Click.

Sam sat silently with the phone glued to his ear, despite the fact that no one was on the other end. Two arbitrary clicks, a buzz, and some silence later, he finally hung the receiver back up on the night stand.

Sam got up from the bed and leaned his ear up to the bathroom door where he could hear the shower still running.

"Hey, Cathy?"

There was no response from the bathroom. Sam furrowed his brow. "Cathy, are you still showering?" The water was loud, maybe she couldn't hear him. He tried the doorknob and found it locked.

195

"Fuck."

Sam scanned the room—the curtains, the TV, the coffee maker, the familiar pile of luggage. Then he noticed a piece of hotel stationary folded in half on top of the room mini-fridge. He picked up the paper and unfolded it. The Boomtown Hotel & Casino letterhead glared back at him from the top, and underneath, scribbled handwriting stretched the length of the paper.

It wasn't a letter; it was the lyrics to a song or poem. Sam felt as though he was prying, but he read it anyway.

I sank into the river's flow
and held on with all my might
caught in the undertow
like disappearing light
I stumbled into this
with legs unfit to stand
swing and then a miss
but reaching for my hand
Big green eyes
Big green eyes
There were so many days
where morning turned to night
and all that I could say
was it's gonna be alright

Big green eyes

Big green eyes

Big green eyes

And I never let it show

But it kills me trying to hide

But only the river knows

Where the water will divide

Big green eyes

Big green eyes

Big green eyes

A loud THUMP from the bathroom jolted Sam out of his daze. He quickly folded the stationary, set it down, and rushed back to the bathroom door.

"Hey, I heard a noise. You okay?" Again, Sam heard nothing but the sound of water hitting porcelain. Sam stepped back from the bathroom door and pondered his next move. He checked the door knob again as if it might have magically unlocked itself. It hadn't.

"Cathy!" Sam yelled, as he pounded on the door. There was no audible response from the bathroom. Sam took a step back and lifted his size-thirteen boot into the air. The bathroom door was no match—with one swift kick it flew inward. The shower curtain was closed. A large bottle of shampoo had fallen onto the tile floor. Sam whipped the curtain back. Cathy lay naked and motionless in a tub full of water, her mouth and nose just below the surface, clearly not conscious.

"Oh my God, no no no no no no no." Sam repeated, frantically pulling her from the water. A wave of water rolled out of the tub as Sam pulled Cathy over the edge and onto the cold tile floor. "Stay with me, goddammit," Sam pleaded. He checked her nose and mouth for signs of breathing while simultaneously checking her pulse. There was nothing. She was turning blue. Life was leaving her body, and Sam knew it. He clasped his hands together and placed them in between her breasts, administering quick, repetitive chest compressions. Sam checked her breathing again, still nothing. He returned to chest compressions, pushing violently downward in a rapid, manic fashion.

"Fuck!" he screamed. Tremors rolled through his arms and legs as the patient grew colder by the second. He glared at the phone, a mile away, and he knew by the time paramedics arrived it would be too late. It was already too late. Sam leaned over Cathy's face, tilted her neck back, pinched her nose, then wrapped his mouth around her cold, blue lips. Five breaths later he came up for air and continued chest compressions.

After more mouth-to-mouth, Sam gave chest compressions one more try. His arms were failing him now and his shoulders had turned numb from the physical exertion. He hadn't even begun to fathom what losing Cathy would mean to him, or to his journey. All he felt was regret. Regret that he had allowed this woman to die right in front of him. Regret that he couldn't save her. Regret that he had opened himself up to her at all. Regret that he had allowed himself to be vulnerable after carrying around a sleeping bag full of nothing but socks and sadness for the last eight years. Loss wasn't just a black cloud that dumped rain onto Sam every waking moment, it was a fucking freight train that found a way to impale him no matter which side of the tracks he ran on.

On what seemed like the 500th chest compression, Cathy's head suddenly lurched up from the tile and spewed a janitor's bucket full of soapy water into the air, onto the tile, and all over Sam.

"Cathy!" Sam cried. A flurry of violent coughs and hacks followed. Cathy's eyes grew so wide that tears simultaneously streamed out of them, as if water was finding its way out of every possible orifice. Sam lifted Cathy up to a sitting position as she continued to cough up more water and saliva and phlegm and wine and whatever food was still in her stomach from dinner. Her senses shot, Cathy began to shiver on the tile.

"Here," Sam said, grabbing a towel. "You need to warm up." Sam wrapped the thin, white, motel-issue towel around Cathy's shoulders and dried her as gently as he could. "What were you doing in here?"

199

The shock of sudden conscious coupled with a throat torn to shreds, Cathy couldn't respond verbally. She just stared at Sam through thankful, bloodshot eyes.

#

Sam sat on the edge of Cathy's bed and watched her eat a large serving of chocolate mousse out of a crystal wine glass, courtesy of the fine folks at room service. Cathy hadn't said much in the last hour, and Sam didn't want her throat to hurt any worse than it probably already did. He got up off the bed and wandered to the mini-fridge.

"Is there anything I can get you?" Sam asked.

Cathy mimed smoking a cigarette. Sam turned his head. "You're kidding me right." Cathy's straight face didn't waver. "You're not kidding. Okay. I can't believe you want a cigarette." Cathy offered a half-smile.

Ten minutes later, Sam returned with a pack of Marlboro Lights in a soft pack that he'd paid eleven fucking dollars for at the gift shop in the lobby. He'd forgotten to buy a lighter, but found matches in the room. Cathy lit a cigarette in her bed and took a sip of wine from a hotel glass. Sam watched her, amazed at her resiliency.

"What were you doing in there?" Sam asked. He wanted to know. He needed to know. He studied her in her tank top and cotton panties. "Don't talk," he added. "You shouldn't talk."

"I want you to fuck me," Cathy said plainly and directly, like she was ordering a pizza.

Sam was taken aback.

"I want you to come over here. I want it."

"What?"

Cathy finished her wine and her cigarette and placed them both on the night stand. She slid the covers down to her feet and repositioned herself on an oversized pillow. Her eyes locked with Sam's and she slowly opened her legs for him. She reached for his hand and pulled him toward her. She unbuckled his belt and slid his jeans down to his knees. She slipped her hands inside his boxer shorts and found him ready. She pulled him closer until he was on top, and then inside of her.

"Pin my arms back," Cathy demanded.

"Do what?"

"I want to be held down. Hold me down."

Sam hesitated but obeyed her command, pinning her arms down on the bed by her wrists. "Go hard please," she instructed. "I want to feel all of you." Six minutes of thrusting and unspeakable, metaphysical connection followed. Cathy came once, and then again, her eyes locked into Sam's as he held her wrists down hard enough to leave an imprint in the memory foam mattress.

"Where do you want me to finish?" Sam asked, on the verge. Cathy grabbed the back of his head and pulled his face into the crook of her neck.

"Just keep going," she moaned.

Sam finished strong, emptying himself inside of her. He then collapsed and let out a deep exhale, the kind of breath that escapes when you haven't made love in almost a decade.

CHAPTER 18

Cathy woke up two hours earlier than Sam the next morning, a reversal that felt strange even to her. Clad in only a tank top and panties, she pulled the curtains open just enough to see the sun cast long shadows along the gas pumps at the Chevron station across the street. She looked back at Sam, passed out on his stomach in a jungle of linens.

Cathy clicked open the clasps on Sam's guitar case as quietly as she could and pulled out the Gibson. Sam's bed creaked as she sat down on the corner and slid the guitar into playing position. She rested her chin against the body, letting her stringy blonde hair trickle down the sides. She wrapped her hand around the neck as her fingers found the rosewood fret board. She plucked quietly – almost silently. A song for Sam as he slept so soundly.

#

A bevy of familiar belongings sat crammed in the backseat of the Monte Carlo as it motored through Louisiana: Cathy's Texas Rangers bag and Sam's bag of the sleeping variety, a beloved bonsai tree, and two guitar cases – one with the mighty Gibson and the other with a beater guitar full of cash. Sam rode shotgun with his stack of dog-eared records in his lap. He had no reason to carry them so close, but there they were. He patted his shirt pocket to make sure something else was there – the envelope with the letter that told him to "stop sending money." Today would be the day he would get the answers to his questions.

The pair was a little more than halfway to their final destination, California, and Sam could see in Cathy's eyes that all the driving was beginning to wear her down. As they crossed the border from Louisiana into Texas Cathy snuck a glance at Sam and could see anticipation in his eyes. She wished like hell she knew what was so important to him here. Their route would take them into Dallas, and then straight south to Houston. As they approached the Dallas-Fort Worth metroplex, the interstate became more congested, and by the time they could spot downtown in the distance, the Monte Carlo had slowed to a crawl. Cathy wondered if it was a sign. That if Sam felt trapped on this concrete long enough, he'd realize that his best option was to keep moving forward, through Texas, head down, eyes forward. Cathy shook her head, she could be a little too poetic at times.

As the Monte Carlo finally slogged through downtown Dallas in bumper-to-bumper traffic, Sam glared up at the skyscrapers that surrounded him and suddenly felt very small. He wished that the car could go faster, away from the buildings. He briefly wondered if he could make it through downtown on foot faster than in the car. He imagined himself with his thumb in the air somewhere in south Dallas as the Monte Carlo caught up with him. He pictured Cathy rolling down the window just long enough to flip him off before continuing down the road. He imagined never seeing her again. Texas had that effect on him. It also made him tired.

"What happened to you last night?" Sam asked, breaking a solid hour of silence. "Seriously. What were you doing?"

"You don't get to ask that," Cathy replied sharply, catching Sam off guard. "Not right now."

"I'm sorry," Sam said. "I guess you just fell asleep."

"I went under the water and you pulled me out," Cathy offered. "Let's leave it at that."

The Monte Carlo puttered south on Interstate 45 through a bevy of small, nothing-to-see-here Texas towns with names like Ferris, Palmer and Ennis. On the other side of Corsicana, the land opened up and the towns became few and far between.

Sam began to feel his eyes grow heavy after seeing the umpteenth billboard for the same truck stop somewhere in Huntsville. In Madisonville, the Monte Carlo hit a rainstorm that threw sheets of rain at the windshield sideways. Raindrops the size of bullets pummeled the glass but somehow didn't break it. The flurry only lasted a few minutes, and when it ceased Cathy could feel her heart beating through her chest. She glanced down at her speedometer. She was only driving 35, but so was everyone else on the road.

The rainstorm passed, but a blanket of mist remained for miles and miles. It was the kind of rain that you couldn't even feel if you were standing in it, but it created a frost-like pattern on the windshield that required intermittent use of the wipers, which hadn't been replaced since God only knew when.

As they neared Houston, Cathy noticed that Sam had fallen asleep with his head pressed against the passenger window. In his lap he held one of his records—the John Prine album with the young man sitting on the stacks of hay. In the upper right hand corner was a round orange sticker that read "Promotional Copy. Not For Sale." Cathy slid the record out of his grasp and turned it over. The back was white and contained a blurb written by Kris Kristofferson. At the top, the track listing displayed thirteen songs. As soon as she scanned them, she wished she hadn't.

The title of track number five on Side A was "Sam Stone."

#

The Monte Carlo was rumbling over asphalt but Cathy didn't know where she was or how long she had been driving. Her nerves were shot and her heart was barely beating. To top it off, the man sitting next to her—whatever his name was—was still asleep.

Cathy didn't remember driving through Huntsville, Conroe, or New Waverly. She had weaved her way through downtown Houston on autopilot, without stopping. She had driven through the big city two hours ago, and she figured she would just keep driving until the road crumbled into dirt or her tires fell flat, or the Monte Carlo ran out of gas, whichever happened first. She sputtered into Galveston on fumes, with the road both literally and figuratively running out in front of her. She had reached the Gulf of Mexico. There was no interstate left to carry her any further. Night had fallen. With the ocean in front of her, Cathy pulled to a stop and killed the car's engine.

#

When Sam awoke, he found himself alone in a dark car in an unfamiliar setting. He rolled the passenger window down and breathed in the kind of humidity that only gulf air can provide. He rubbed his eyes, trying to adjust them to this new darkness—but it was the kind of nighttime that convinces you the sun will never shine again.

Sam unbuckled his seat belt and gazed out the windshield. There was a line of wooden posts connected by sections of thick rope about twenty yards away. Beyond the posts he could see nothing but sand fading into the shadows of the deep, black ocean. He stared out as far as he could, catching intermittent glimpses of a flashing light somewhere in the middle of it all, miles away.

As the sound of endless waves rolling and crashing against rocks filled his ears, Sam began to make sense of his surroundings. He had been here before. In fact, much of his childhood had been spent on this very beach, but now, in the still of twilight, it appeared completely foreign to him. The beach was lit by a single street light that came from somewhere behind the car. A lonely lifeguard tower stood nearby, abandoned until morning. Sam scanned the beach again, spotting a figure standing in the wet sand at the water's edge. It was a woman, and that woman was smoking a cigarette. Sam squinted at the figure standing alone in the dark. "Cathy?" he called out. He watched the orange glow of the cigarette flicker and go dark as it landed in the sand. The figure turned and stopped, then crept toward him in a direct line. It was indeed a woman, and as she grew closer, Sam was relieved to discover that it was, in fact, Cathy.

"What are we doing in Galveston?" Sam asked. Cathy stepped over a section of rope and continued toward Sam.

"What's your real name?" Cathy asked. The lone street light cast haunting shadows under her eyes.

"What are you talking about?" Sam asked. Cathy dove into the car and retrieved the John Prine record. She pressed the record into his chest, then took two steps back and folded her arms. "Side A. Song five."

Sam turned the record over and scanned it, but he already knew what he was going to find. He glared at the waves as if the answers might somehow come rolling in with the rising tide.

"I'll just leave you here and let you figure it out, then." Cathy said. She walked back toward the car and opened the back hatch, then began pulling Sam's items from the car.

"What are you doing?" Sam asked.

"Getting your stuff out of here." Cathy said, grabbing his sleeping bag and dragging it out onto the asphalt below.

"Cathy, wait," Sam insisted. Cathy continued to funnel Sam's items onto the gravel below with reckless abandon. She slammed the trunk and opened the driver's side door, her keys in hand. Sam let out a deep breath and stared at the sea.

"It's Alan Walker."

Cathy stopped short of getting in. She stared at Sam.

"Who is Alan Walker?"

"Can we just go somewhere and talk? I can explain."

"Go where, *Alan*? We're here. This is where we are. This is where the road has taken us." She spied the ramshackle lifeguard stand over her shoulder. The tide slipped in and around its peeling wooden legs every few seconds, never ceasing to invade and then recede back into its depths.

#

"Do you remember that accident I told you about?" Sam asked Cathy as the pair sat in complete darkness in matching lifeguard chairs, gazing out at a black ocean that filled their ears with soft chaos.

"The chin injury," she replied.

"Yeah... here's the... I don't know how to say this without sounding crazy..."

"Just say it."

"I used to be... a lifetime ago... I was a doctor."

The waves crashed against the jagged cliffs on Galveston bay.

"Are you kidding me?

"I'm not kidding you."

"What kind of doctor?"

"I was a surgeon."

Cathy laughed. "Well, that explains the stitching skills." She turned to look at him but couldn't see him, he was lost in all that darkness, a sinner in a makeshift confessional.

"I was in my first year of residency when it happened."

"The accident?"

"Yes. I'd been up almost two whole days. I'd just completed an appendectomy. I don't even remember it. I don't remember getting in my car. I don't remember driving. I only remember waking up."

"So you hurt your chin and you changed your name?"

Sam took a deep breath and held it in. His eyes traveled out beyond the point where ocean met the sky, he could almost make out stars. He let out the breath, slowly.

"I hurt more than my chin. I hurt people."

"What happened, Sam?" Cathy said, refusing to call him Alan. She felt close to him again, if only for this moment.

"There were two boys," Sam said, his voice cracking. "They were playing in their yard. I hit them... I ran them over. They were seven and nine years old. They never grew any older than that."

"Sam..." Cathy searched in the darkness for Sam's hand, finding it shaking and trembling. She wanted so desperately to release the dozens of tears that suddenly flooded her eyes, but she held them in for Sam. This was his time to cry. She wouldn't take that away from him. She was glad it was pitch black. His voice was enough. She squeezed his hand tightly—Morse code, to let him know that she understood. God, did she understand. She couldn't hold the tears in much longer, so she released the air from her lungs instead. Sam felt her grip intensify, squeezing his hand so hard that it hurt, like she might be holding on to something for the last time.

"I have secrets, Sam."

"Do you want to tell them to me?

"I can't."

An eternity passed. Cathy's wet eyes danced back and forth in the darkness, desperate to make out Sam's face. "Can I ask you something?"

"Yes," Sam said.

"You remember the day we met... in the cemetery?"

"Of course."

Cathy continued... "You said you were going to come back the next day to finish Ollie's marker... Well, I came back the next day and waited for you but you never showed up. Why didn't you come?"

Sam's mind raced as he attempted to recall the evening. "I don't know," he said. "I guess I forgot. I'm so sorry."

"No, it's okay."

"No. It's not." Sam folded his fingers into hers. "I promise you, I will finish it, one day. I promise you that."

"Please don't make me any promises," Cathy said as another wave crashed into the lifeguard stand, pushing hundreds of gallons of water beneath them but refusing to carry them away.

#

The tide had come in, and Sam and Cathy sat on the hood of the Monte Carlo as Cathy aimlessly plucked the strings on the Gibson while Sam watched, entranced.

"You gonna write a song for me someday?" Sam asked, half-joking.

"Maybe I already have," Cathy responded. Cathy laid the guitar down gently on the hood and approached Sam, wrapping her arms around his neck. "So tell me, why the name Sam Stone?" she asked, their lips inches apart.

Sam considered the question and realized there was only one way to answer it.

"I guess I just thought it had a nice ring to it."

Cathy leaned in and kissed him as the ocean howled in the distance.

213

CHAPTER 19

The sun rose fast and fiery the next morning, and much to Cathy's chagrin, the drive from Galveston to Houston was quicker than advertised. Traffic was light, and the sun bounced off of downtown Houston's towering steel buildings in the distance. Cathy eyed Sam, lost in thought, as reflective as the skyscrapers that grew closer with every passing second. Apart from the occasional homeless person or jogger, the city seemed to still be asleep. Not Sam. He was wide awake.

With Sam navigating, Cathy exited the highway in the middle of downtown, maneuvering through the heart of the city before roaming its fringes. The Monte Carlo entered an old neighborhood just out of the shadows of the tall buildings. "Make a right here," Sam said, and Cathy obliged, driving past a

Catholic church and then an elementary school surrounded by a chain link fence. Sam's eyes shimmered as the memories flooded back in.

"Another right," he said, and then they found themselves in a neighborhood of small, once modest homes now gentrified by rich white assholes driving Infinitis and Porsche SUV's.

"That one up there," Sam instructed, his eyes widening. He pointed at a house with peeling yellow paint and ankle-high grass sandwiched between two upscale remodels—the one bad apple in the bunch. Cathy drove closer. "Don't park right in front, though," Sam said. "Right here is good."

Cathy pulled up along the curb two houses down and cut off the engine. She gazed out at the house, curious. "Who lives there?" she asked.

Sam let out a deep breath. "That's the house I grew up in. It didn't used to look like that. It used to look alive. It hasn't looked alive in years."

Cathy contemplated taking off her seat belt. "Do you want me to go with you, or wait here, or…?"

Sam's eyes were glued to the house and his mind was churning.

"Sam?" Cathy asked again. His gaze remained on the house.

"I think you should go on ahead to California," he said. The words hit Cathy like a cannon in the middle of her chest. Sam

215

looked at her, finally, and continued, "I'll catch up with you in a couple of days."

Whatever walls Cathy had let down for Sam suddenly built up again in an instant. She was truly at a loss. She wanted to scream, but she remained silent and controlled. Her army had rebuilt her defense and she was fast becoming a stranger.

"Are you okay?" he asked.

"No, you're right. I should go," Cathy said. She reached in the back, took some money out of her guitar case, and handed it to him.

"You might need some of this," she said.

"Cathy no, I'm not taking this."

"Sam, don't do this. Don't be a martyr. Take it." She pried open his hand and laid the money inside it, then folded it back up.

Sam stared out the windshield, his emotions stirring. He looked over at Cathy who was staring a hole through the steering wheel. "You should probably go now," she finally said.

Sam refused to make a move. Suddenly, he didn't want to be in Houston at all. He wanted to stay in the car, go to sleep, and let Cathy drive him far away from this place. He wanted no control over his own destiny. Fuck destiny.

Cathy broke her stare on the steering wheel and looked silently at Sam one more time. Sam knew those eyes. They were the same eyes he had glimpsed in that hearse a month ago. Only now, they were dancing.

"Kiss me and then get out of the car," Cathy insisted, like a parent ordering a child. Sam obeyed her command, and moved in for a quick, soft kiss on the lips. It was non-romantic, but it was a button. A signal. A punctuation. And with it, Sam retrieved his sleeping bag, guitar case, records, and bonsai tree, then climbed out of the car and touched down on the sidewalk.

The car revved, then idled. "Hey Sam," Cathy called out from the car. Sam turned around.

"All these things that you carry around with you... maybe they're just slowing you down."

Sam looked down at his belongings, unsure of what to say next.

Cathy continued... "Whatever it is that you're looking for here, I don't think you're going to find it. I think it evaporated a long time ago. I think it lives in the sky, and in your head."

Sam looked back at the house in the distance, then turned back to Cathy. "You may be right."

Sam reached down and picked up his guitar case, then moved towards the car. He opened the passenger door and slid the case inside.

"I want you to keep this," Sam said. Cathy glared in shock. "I'm never going to play it like you do."

"Sam, I can't take your grandpa's guitar," Cathy said.

"It's yours now," Sam insisted. He ducked out of the car and shut the door, catching one last glimpse of Cathy in the driver's seat.

"I hope I find you," he said.

"You're a coward, Sam."

Cathy threw the car into drive and slammed the gas. Tires squealed against asphalt, and a shell-shocked Sam stared as the Monte Carlo burned down the block and ran a stop sign. Cathy hung a left and was gone. Sam held his gaze until he could no longer hear the rumble of the Monte Carlo's mighty V8. When it was gone, all that remained was the vacant hum of a distant highway and the chirp of a nearby blue jay.

Sam's feet felt heavy as he labored toward the house. He stopped on the sidewalk in front and examined a rusted black mailbox with reflective numbers reading "402" adhered to the side. He examined the house in all its crumbling glory. The place had really gone to shit, even more so than the last time he had been there, back when it was just starting to go to shit. The shutters were faded and cracked now. A loose gutter lay broken and alone on the ground next to some overgrown bushes. A forgotten sprinkler sat in the middle of the yard with eight inches of grass grown through its top.

In the middle of this garden of sadness, a shiny black Cadillac Escalade sat parked in the driveway. Sam scanned it as he scuttled up the driveway toward the front door. When he reached it he discovered the screen door was already flapped open, so he gave three quick knocks. There was no answer. Sam's ears filled with deep, pumping bass grooves that emanated from inside the house. His patience growing thin, he slammed his fist on the door multiple times. The music finally stopped and the front door flew open.

"What chu want?" a small, sweaty man in a wife beater asked. Sam towered over the man by at least a foot, maybe more. The man held a peeled banana in one hand a television remote in the other. Despite these non-threatening accessories, his stare meant business.

"I'm looking for Gary," Sam said, craning his neck to get a quick look around the living room, which was cluttered with boxes and clothing and God knows what else.

"Gary lives in the back," the man said, looking Sam up and down. "Who are you?"

"Out back?"

The man stuck his thumb in the air and pointed it over his shoulder. "In the fuckin' guest house."

Sam was perplexed. To his knowledge, there was no guest house on the property.

219

"Okay, thanks," Sam muttered as he backed away and narrowly avoided stepping in a boot-sized hole in the front porch. "Hey, is that your car?" Sam asked before the man could close the door.

"Shit, I wish, dude. That's Gary's."

Sam stepped off the porch and walked around to the back where he greeted a waist-high, chain-link fence. Deep in the backyard, where the garage had once been, stood a ramshackle guest house. In front of it sat a rusted 1978 Ford Ranger pickup with only a fraction of its original sea foam green paint remaining.

"Mother fucker," Sam growled. Sam scaled the fence with little problem and then darted toward the guest house on a mission. Before he could get to the front door the damn thing opened. Gary stepped out. He was the same height as Sam, but much skinnier. He was shirtless, wearing only a faded pair of Budweiser sleep pants.

"Alan," Gary said. "What are you doing here?"

"What are *you* doing here?" Sam echoed.

"I live here."

"Who's that guy living in the house?"

"You met Froggy? Yeah, he rents the house. He sells stereos."

"You're living in the garage and renting out the house?"

"Hey man, don't throw your shit on me."

Sam eyeballed the truck in the yard. "Fuck's sake, Gary. Why is Loretta rusting in the fucking yard?"

"I had to take it out of the garage when I converted it. It doesn't even run." Gary motioned toward the guest house. "Do you want to come in? I got some Townhouse crackers and shit." Sam ripped the envelope from his pocket, yanked out the letter and slammed it against Gary's sweaty, bare chest.

"What does this mean?"

Gary slid the letter off his chest and scanned it. His memory jogged. "Oh. Yeah, man. The fuckin' cops showed up a couple of weeks ago. Thought I was selling drugs. I can't have envelopes with cash showing up at my house twice a week."

"Did you stop selling drugs, Gary? I wasn't aware."

"Hey fuck you, man, I make an honest living. I haven't even seen you in, like, nine years. You can't just show up at my house…"

Sam pressed closer toward Gary. "You didn't even give her the money, did you?"

"Hey man, I held up my end of the bargain."

"Really? Where does she live?"

Gary stared into the yard without an answer. Sam pushed further, his anger pulsing.

"Tell me where you've been taking the thousands of dollars I've been sending for the last eight years. Tell me, Gary."

Gary remained a statue. Sam's face burst with redness. "You can't tell me because you don't know!"

Gary finally broke. "I gave her the money, at first. Okay? But she wouldn't accept it. She doesn't want your fuckin' money, man."

"So you just kept it? Is that how you bought that monstrosity in the driveway? With my hard-earned money?" Sam grabbed Gary's collarbone, putting him in a vice grip. Gary's knees buckled.

"Chill the fuck out, bro. I saved some of it."

Sam released Gary from his grip and stormed past him in a blind rage toward the guest house. Sam then slammed his fist through a plate glass window in the converted garage.

"What the hell are you doing?" Gary screamed. Sam retrieved his arm from the shattered pane, his knuckles and lower arm completely covered in blood. He glared back at Gary.

"Give me the keys."

"You broke my window, dude."

"Give me the fucking keys!"

"You're not taking my Escalade, bro."

"THE KEYS TO THE TRUCK, GARY."

"I told you, it doesn't run." Gary stared at Sam's hand as blood gushed out in spurts and dribbles. Sam seemed unaffected, numb. Gary slowly backed into the guest house. Sam turned around to see Froggy standing on the back porch.

"You fuck up your hand, dude?" Froggy asked nonchalantly. Sam stared at Froggy silently as the blood continued to geyser from his wrist. He turned back around as Gary re-emerged from the guest house, keys in hand. "Why don't you let me take you to a hospital?"

Sam snatched the keys from Gary's hand. "I'm a doctor, Gary."

Froggy stood closer now, suddenly topless. He handed his tank top to Sam, who politely took it with his left hand. "Thank you, Froggy."

Sam wrapped the fabric around his hand, tourniquet style, then unlocked the truck's driver's side door and yanked it open. He climbed in, stuck the key in the ignition, and cranked the engine on the first try.

Gary shrugged at Froggy. "Is he gonna be okay?" Froggy asked.

"I guess we'll find out," Gary responded.

Sam threw the truck into first gear, but before he could leave, Gary called out. "Alan!" Sam rolled the window down, his face draining of color.

"Last I heard she was living in Cotton Mouth, on the other side of Bayville. She's married again."

Sam stared out the windshield, punched the accelerator and mowed through the yard, barreling over the chain link fence, and narrowly missing the Escalade in the driveway. The truck swerved wildly into the street where Sam promptly smashed into a utility pole and passed out at the wheel.

CHAPTER 20

Alan Walker woke up in a small recovery room on the fourth floor of Houston's St. John's Hospital with an IV in his arm and an incessant beep in his ear. The TV perched high in the corner of the room played a barely-audible episode of "Jeopardy." Based on this, Alan knew it was sometime between four o'clock and five o'clock. It was only then that he realized he was not the only person in the room. Sitting in the corner, in a blue uphol-stered chair that had seen better days, was his wife Lydia. She had earned every one of her twenty-nine years, and today she wore a beige summer dress with birds on it. She wore no makeup, but she beamed even without it. Alan could tell by her face that she had been crying. She was always crying about something.

Lydia stood up, relieved that Alan had awoken, but this was not a time to smile or breathe too deeply or celebrate. Alan flashed back to the accident scene and the sight of those two children receiving CPR. The images flooded his mind like a tidal wave.

"My God, you're awake," Lydia said, pulling him out of his own thoughts for a precious moment.

"Did they make it?" he asked her. Lydia pulled a tissue out of her purse and sniffled, mustering a mere head shake before the tears started again.

Alan discovered the IV in his arm and then glanced over at the bag delivering Atavan into his bloodstream in incremental drips. He closed his eyes tight, and with a single grimaced yank, he ripped the medical device out of his arm and tossed it onto the cold, sticky floor.

"Alan, what are you doing—"

"Let's go. Please. Let's just go."

Alan tore past Lydia without so much as a hug or embrace and headed straight for the door. It opened and closed with two clicks, leaving Lydia alone.

Rain drizzled onto the cement and automobiles as Lydia tracked Alan into the hospital's parking lot. "Where are you going?" she asked.

"I'm going home."

226

"Alan, stop. You're not walking home."

"I'm not walking, I'm driving."

"Your car isn't here, Alan." Lydia finally caught him from behind, grabbing his hand and spinning him around. Alan glared at his wife. He wanted to cry, but he didn't. He couldn't. She tried desperately to meet his eyes but they were somewhere else, darting around the parking lot, looking for something.

"Where is your car?" he finally asked.

The ride home was silent, as was the remainder of the evening. The silence stretched into days as Alan turned more and more inward. The accident was ruled just that—an accident. Fatigue was the culprit, according to the police report, and because Alan had no drugs or alcohol in his system, he wasn't charged with any sort of crime. It was all just one big terrible tragedy. The boys had died instantly from blunt force trauma the moment Alan's car made impact with them.

Alan was forced to take a three-month leave of absence from his duties at the hospital. Initially, he pushed against the decision, desperately wanting to return to work, if only as a distraction. But even he understood that a distracted surgeon was a dangerous surgeon.

A civil suit followed, and Alan didn't have the strength to fight it. A judge awarded the family a $400,000 settlement. Insurance took the brunt of it, but Alan's savings account was completely depleted by the end of it all.

As the months wore on, Alan's interest in returning to his medical practice faded into nothingness. He was no longer a person who felt things. He became a witness to other people's emotions, refusing to absorb them or allow them into his own body.

Lydia couldn't accept this cold, detached person as the new Alan. She held on for months, surviving on nothing but hope. Hope that he would wake up one morning and smile at her, or bring her coffee, or ask her if she wanted to go on one of their strolls around the neighborhood. That was the Alan she knew. The Alan she'd married. The Alan she loved. The new Alan slept until noon and spent afternoons drinking coffee in the backyard while listening to an AM radio that spewed static-filled religious sermons from parts unknown.

With their finances in shambles, Lydia was forced to take a job as an office manager for a local chiropractor. It was enough money to pay the utility bills and buy groceries, but nowhere near enough to keep up with the mortgage on a four-bedroom, three-thousand square foot house. Foreclosure soon followed, forcing Alan and Lydia to move into a one-bedroom apartment.

Not long after the move, Alan's grandfather died. It was expected, but the death still shook Alan to his core. Alan received a nominal cash amount from his grandfather's will in addition to a stack of old vinyl records, a bonsai tree, and a guitar. Alan found solace and meaning in the items, and attached serious sentimental value to them, despite the fact that he had spent little time with his grandfather during his life. His obsession with the items was not lost on Lydia, who desperately craved some sort of affection from her husband. But this wasn't a man she even recognized anymore.

It had been six months since there had been any sort of closeness, but then one night, it happened: two strangers made love. It was short and Alan came quickly, but the brief physical contact after so many months gave Lydia hope that there might be a light at the end of the tunnel.

The next morning, Lydia came home from work to discover that the records, the guitar and the bonsai tree were missing. So was Alan. He had simply disappeared. There was no note explaining his absence, just two crisp $100 bills on the kitchen counter next to an AM radio emitting static.

CHAPTER 21

Sam Stone woke up in a small recovery room on the fourth floor of Houston's St. John's Hospital with a thick layer of gauze wrapped around his right arm from his elbow to his wrist. Distant beeps and chatter droned from a nearby nurse's station. A small flat screen TV above his bed played an episode of "Judge Judy" in the wrong aspect ratio. Sam's eyes shifted down to a wingback chair in the corner of the room. It was empty. There was no one waiting for him. It was only after this realization that Sam felt the pain in his arm. Even the slightest movement triggered shockwaves that rolled through his central nervous system. There were no IVs in his arm and no machines dripping anything.

"FUCK," Sam said with a wince as he worked his right leg over to the side of the bed. He was attempting a jail break.

"Going somewhere?" a voice said from behind a small curtain. Sam looked up to see a doctor with a white soul patch that perfectly matched his white lab coat. A bronze name tag identified him as "Dr. Davey."

"Yeah, I'm leaving," Sam replied.

"You have sixteen stitches in your left arm and you're under a good deal of sedation. Please lie back down."

"Who brought me here?"

"Two men, one tall, one short. The tall one said he was a relative. They didn't stay."

Flustered, Sam shook his head. "You know, I used to work here. I was the best surgeon in this place."

Dr. Davey laughed and gently pushed Sam back down onto the bed by his shoulder. "Painkillers make us feel all kinds of things, don't they? Rest up now, okay? We'll probably discharge you in two or three hours."

"Three hours? For stitches in my arm?"

"Well, a surgeon of your caliber would know that we don't discharge patients who are still under observation, especially those with the amount of hydrocodone that you currently have in your system. Did you know have a small perforation in your right ear drum?"

"Why would you need to look into my ear?"

Defeated, sedated, and in serious pain, Sam leaned his head back against his pillow and resigned himself to watching "Judge Judy."

Two hours and thirty-six minutes later, Sam was discharged and given a sheet of paper to take to the billing clerk on the way out. Sam scanned the detailed breakdown of expenses that he had rung up during his six-hour visit, but he didn't even make it to the bottom of the page. It was bound to be more money than he had, so he quietly folded the piece of paper and stuck it in his shirt pocket.

Sam took the long route to the billing department, winding through the women's center and children's wing before coming across a pair of familiar double doors that read "SURGERY. Authorized Personnel Only." Sam scanned the empty hall and peered into an equally bare waiting room, his curiosity getting the better of him. He quietly pushed through the doors and found himself in his old stomping grounds. The place looked smaller, like a childhood home rediscovered as an adult, but the sounds and smells were exactly the same.

Sam had lived and breathed the air trapped in these walls— stale oxygen forced through vents stale with sweat, regret, death. The cold tile floor felt just as sticky as it ever had. Sam's eyes followed its repeating pattern of squares down an endless corridor, past rooms where people received new hearts and lungs,

232

battles were won, and sometimes, lives were lost. But none of it mattered now, as Sam stared into a break room filled with lockers and vending machines. A man in scrubs sat on a bench eating a candy bar, his back turned to Sam. The man turned and caught a glimpse of Sam standing in the doorway in his worn denim shirt and jeans.

"Are you lost?" the man asked, standing up urgently. Sam instantly recognized him. It was Levi, his old friend from medical school. Sam darted for the double doors.

"Hey! Hang on a second!" Levi exclaimed as Sam whooshed through the metal doors back into the main hallway. Sam's steps quickened as he wound through the labyrinth of halls, through the cafeteria, past the gift shop, until he reached the billing department. He glanced behind him, assured that he had lost Levi, retrieved the folded bill from his pocket and gave it to the billing clerk, an apathetic woman in her early twenties with a lip ring.

"Your insurance card?" she asked with the least amount of volume and enthusiasm required by law.

"No insurance," Sam replied. The clerk rolled her eyes without actually rolling them, a skill she had perfected in hundreds of conversations identical to this one. She clicked and clacked on her computer so long that Sam wondered if she might be playing Tetris instead.

"It's $1,885.34."

The clerk glared at Sam with dead eyes. Sam glared back, thinking about the money that Cathy had given him. He had no desire to spend a single penny of it here. He shouldn't have even stopped at the billing office. He could've easily left the hospital and never returned. It wouldn't be the first debt he'd run from, but something was different now. He was sick and tired of running from his debts.

"Alan?" Sam turned and saw Levi standing at the end of the hall. He took a few steps closer, trying to get a better look at Sam's face. "Holy shit, it is you."

The medical clerk let out a loud sigh.

"My God, what are you doing here?" Levi asked with wide, curious eyes. Sam lifted his arm up, wincing as the pain shot through it.

"Accident."

Levi grabbed Sam's bill from the medical clerk, scanning it intensely. "Code thirty four this one."

"His bill is one thousand—"

"I don't care what his bill is. Code thirty four it."

"Levi, it's okay," Sam insisted. "I'll pay it."

"Bull shit."

"He said he could pay it," the clerk chimed in.

"You don't know who this is, okay? CODE THIRTY FOUR IT."

The clerk shook her head and clicked and clacked some more. "People get fired for shit like this," she mumbled under her breath.

Levi took in Sam, blown away that he was standing before him after all this time. "Do you need a ride somewhere?"

#

Sam found his back and legs perfectly contoured to the soft, supple confines of a leather passenger seat in Levi's Range Rover. He closed his eyes and soaked in the comfort as his bonsai tree bounced gently in his lap. Levi steered the luxury SUV through Houston traffic, occasionally glancing over at Sam. The sun flooded through the windshield onto Sam's face, but he didn't mind. The cool, clean air from the A/C vents were refreshing his soul.

"You know it's funny, I brought you up the other day with Brenda," Levi said, interrupting Sam's moment of Zen. "The way you left, it was just so sudden. It's really amazing running into you."

"How is Brenda?" Sam asked, his eyes peeled open just wide enough to see the white highway lines rushing toward him.

"We've been married six years now. Two daughters—three and one."

"That's great, Levi. I'm happy for you." As soon as Sam spoke the words he realized that he meant them, and it made him feel good to know that.

"Jesus, Alan, where have you been all these years?" Levi inquired, almost star struck. Sam pondered the question for a moment, but didn't take long to formulate his response.

"Florida."

"Florida, huh? What's in Florida?" He stared at Sam, studying this new version of him. "Sorry, Alan. It's none of my business."

"It's okay," Sam replied, staring through the branches of the bonsai tree out the windshield where the entire world was open in front of him. He sucked in a chest full of cold air and let it out slowly. "It's kind of a long story, Levi."

"Well, I don't even know where I'm driving you, Alan."

"You know, Lydia and I, after the... it was... you know. Things got ... difficult."

Sam had mumbled a mouthful of nothing much at all, but Levi remained intrigued. "I can imagine so, Alan, I can imagine so."

"She was working for this guy," Sam continued, "Dr. Berry. Some chiropractor out in Deer Park. She'd get off at five and be home by five-fifteen sharp, usually. I liked that. It was consistent. Routine. I needed that." Sam searched the curving road

236

for his next words. Levi might as well have disappeared. Sam was riding shotgun in a driverless vehicle.

"I think it was a Thursday. I made a pizza. DiGiorno. They make a pretty good pizza. It wasn't much, but I made it. It was a little past five when I took it out of the oven. Lydia didn't come home at five-fifteen, like normal, and she didn't come home at five-thirty. When she didn't come home at six I got worried, so I called her. She didn't answer. I called her two more times—straight to her voice mail. I started to feel lost, scared. Very alone. I looked around our apartment at all of our things, you know, just this house full of things all stuffed into an apartment, and I swear, all I could think of was 'goddammit, Lydia, how dare you die and leave me here to deal with all of this? All of this baggage. How dare you make me bury you in the cold, clay soil? How dare you?' I was preparing her funeral in my mind. You know, figuring out who to call first. It was over. I was a widower. Another hour passed and she walks in like nothing had happened. Like I hadn't just buried her six feet in the ground. She was right there, standing in front of me, apologizing because her phone had died and there were two late clients at work. I didn't say anything. I went into the bedroom and I laid down on the bed and I closed my eyes. Later on, she laid down next to me. I could feel the bed move when she slid underneath the covers and went to sleep in the other direction. I decided in that moment that I would never give her another opportunity to put me in that position. To put her in the ground. To go through all those family pictures, to donate her purses and shoes and clothing to charity. To lose her on terms that weren't my own. To grieve her …" Sam stared at the floorboard. "… and goddammit, I've grieved her ever since."

Sam finally caught Levi's glance. Sam shook his head, fully aware that he had just given Levi way more information than he had asked for.

"But to answer your question about Florida … crocodiles," Sam said.

Levi just stared, speechless.

#

The Range Rover pulled into a small gas station on the corner of two farm-to-market roads in the small town of Cotton Mouth, population 2,432. Sam placed his hand on the door handle. "Thanks for the ride, Levi. It was good to see you. I mean it."

Sam climbed out of the passenger seat, leaving behind the comfort of air conditioned luxury for the misery of a humid Houston summer afternoon.

As Sam turned to leave, Levi called out—"Hey Alan!" Sam turned around, sweat already forming on his forehead, his arm blistering underneath an inch and a half of gauze.

"I always thought you got a raw deal," Levi said. Sam studied his shoes and then glanced back into the Range Rover.

"I quit, Levi. I fucking quit."

Levi shrugged and put the Range Rover into reverse, making a left out of the parking lot as Sam watched him speed away. Sam suddenly found himself at literal crossroads, staring blankly at a flashing red light that swung gently in the middle of a quiet intersection. Cotton Mouth was the kind of town where the rattlesnakes ate the grasshoppers and the people ate the rattle snakes. Or so he'd thought. The monstrosity of the city seemed to be closing in on the little town, and mixed in amongst the trailers and ramshackle frame houses, Sam could see new construction going up in the distance. Brick homes. The times they were a changin'.

Sam turned and entered the Turtle Stop gas station, bought a soda and an eight pack of mini donuts, then saddled up to the register.

"Three-oh-eight," the young, pizza-faced clerk mumbled. Sam produced a $100 bill, forcing the teenager to press buttons on the register that he had never touched before. The clerk miraculously gathered ninety-six dollars and some change and dumped it into Sam's hand without even counting it. "Nice bonsai," the clerk said with as much sarcasm as he could muster. Sam stared back at him, his sleeping bag slung over his shoulder, his records under his right arm, and his bonsai tree in his right hand. "You got a phone book?"

The young clerk appeared perplexed by the question. "A what?"

Sam shook his head, stuffed a donut into his mouth and rambled out of the store.

#

An hour later, Sam lumbered down a residential street with a white phone book page in his hand. The sun was in top mid-afternoon form, sending a stream of sweat down Sam's forehead and onto the thin, delicate page. Sam found himself in the area of new construction that he had glimpsed from the convenience store. Sam paced and scanned the numbers on shiny new mail-boxes, eventually stopping. He glared at a house and carefully matched the address on the page to the address on the mailbox. Red brick, one-story, ranch-style. Probably 2,500 square feet. A shiny Lexus SUV sat in the driveway, begging to be driven.

Sam didn't know what to make of this scene. Lydia had clearly moved on and built some sort of life for herself. Sam suddenly convinced himself that he didn't want or need to know anything else. He had traveled halfway across the country, he had arrived, and now it was time to leave. Just as he made this realization, the front flung open and a young boy in a baseball uniform flew toward the SUV in the driveway yelling, "Hurry up mom!"

A shell-shocked Sam dove behind a towering pecan tree in the yard as a familiar voice called out. "Zack, you forgot your glove!" Sam peeked around the tree to see Lydia emerge from the house with a baseball glove in her hand. A short, stocky man followed close behind in a matching uniform that hugged his body in all the wrong places.

Sam scanned the driveway. His Willie Nelson *Shotgun Willie* record sat in the yard by the mailbox, its sleek black vinyl peeking out slightly from its sleeve. "Shit," Sam whispered, realizing that he must have dropped it during his half-baked dive behind the tree.

Sam's attention returned to the SUV when its engine cranked. As it backed out of the driveway, Sam scooted clockwise around the tree like a soldier shifting through a trench. He peered around the tree and saw the SUV halt abruptly at the end of the driveway. The front passenger door flung open and a pair of fat feet stuffed into baseball cleats poked out, one after the other. The stocky man leaned down and picked up the Willie Nelson record, examining it curiously before sliding it under his armpit and returning to the car. The SUV sped away with Lydia in the driver's seat.

241

Sam's eyes followed the tail lights down the block. He was now faced with a choice. Cut his losses or huff it two miles to the youth baseball complex to talk to his ex-wife who had re-married and had a kid. Sam fumbled to his feet and brushed the grass off his clothing. His gaze angled left where the next door neighbor, an old man in a fishing cap and short shorts stared at him suspiciously with a water hose in hand. "It's okay," Sam called out. "I'm just lost." The old man kept watering silently, never taking his eyes off of the stranger in his neighbor's yard.

Sam gathered his belongings and stumbled to the edge of the driveway, looking left and then right. He could see the SUV's brake lights illuminate at a stop sign at the end of the block. As the SUV made a right turn, Sam thought of Cathy, and he wondered why so many people were driving away from him today. He felt alone and road weary. Sam glanced back at the neighbor watering his yard. He was gone. Maybe he'd never existed. Maybe he was Sam, thirty years from now, or thirty years ago. The universe was bizarre in that way. His brain thoroughly scrambled, Sam took a deep breath and began to walk. Somewhere in the distance, the sound of an aluminum baseball bat pinged loudly.

#

By the time Sam made it to the Bayville youth baseball complex, the third inning was winding down. Sam lowered his

242

head and scanned the aging, wooden bleachers that groaned beneath the weight of hot-dog-munching parents. He found Lydia six rows back, his first true glimpse in damn near a decade. Her face hadn't aged, but hair was shorter, an unusual auburn color streaked with blonde highlights. Sam remembered the first time he saw her, sitting across from him waiting on an oil change in a Jiffy Lube. She was reading Time magazine then, she was staring at her smart phone now. She never had liked sports.

"Good eye out there, Parker!" Lydia's husband yelled from the third base line at the batter in the box. Sam rolled his eyes. Of course he was the coach. He had a curious sweat pattern forming under his polyester-clad arms and legs. Large circles of perspiration grew wider by the minute under his pits, and a U-shaped line around his undercarriage formed a sweat saddle.

Sam slid along the brick wall that lined the back of the visitor dugout. This deposited him along a waist-high, chain-link fence near the first base foul line. From there he could see the game without Lydia seeing him. Sam cared little about baseball, but quickly found himself wrapped up in a tie game between the orange team and the purple team. With runners on the corners and two outs, Lydia's son stepped up to the plate. He glared down the third base line at his father, who clapped and confidently shouted "Dig in there, Zacky! Eyes on the ball!" Sam felt

243

a lump grow in his throat as he admired Lydia in the bleachers, now paying full attention to the game. She whistled and clapped, "Go Zack!"

Zack stepped in and took two strikes looking, then swung wildly at a ball in the dirt to end the threat and the inning. He flung his batter's helmet off with a look of dejection and began the somber stagger back to the dugout. There was something odd in the way he stepped that seemed so familiar to Sam. It was his walk. The kid had his gait. Sam quickly did math in his head and something clicked.

As Zack ran into right field at the beginning of the next inning, he made brief eye contact with the stranger leaning against the fence. Sam offered him a crooked smile and Zack flashed one right back. The kid was tall for eight, certainly the tallest on the team, and clearly terrible at sports. Sam looked over at Lydia's husband sitting in the dugout. No way in hell that kid belonged to him. He caught Zack's glance one more time, then slowly backed away from the fence before making his escape.

Sam wandered around the baseball complex for the next half hour and caught glimpses of the game from the safe distance of empty bleachers two fields away. When the game was over, Zack's team had lost 11-7. Sam watched as the purple and orange-clad players crossed the pitcher's mound and slapped hands, muttering "good game," "good game," "good game" until

244

every opposing player had completed the gesture. Sam watched the players disperse, some with their parents, some toward the concession stand where grape snow cones and nachos awaited them. From his vantage point, Sam could see Zack standing next to Lydia's husband, who was speaking to another parent near the dugout. Lydia stood nearby, ready to leave. Eventually, the trio exited the field and entered a parking lot where their SUV awaited.

Sam watched the SUV kick up a cloud of dirt as it rolled out of the lot and made a quick left into a nearby convenience store. Sam sprinted toward the gas station with no plan, just instincts. Bad, bad instincts.

Sam shuffled through the double doors of the packed gas station and looked around. It took a moment before he found the kid in the baseball uniform near the slushee machine. Sam ducked down behind an ice cream freezer to get a better view. It was Zack. Sam got up from his crouched position and stepped slowly toward Zack as the young man dumped a mountain of white frozen liquid into a cup, filling it to the top, then licking off the overflow.

"Nice technique," Sam said genuinely, completely unaware of how creepy and predatory he sounded. Zack turned around and stared at Sam, more confused than afraid.

"I was at the game earlier. I saw you make that catch in right field. Good catch, man."

Zack shrugged and took a slurp of his slushee, "Just luck I guess."

"You like the white cherry slushee?" Sam asked, desperate to make conversation with the kid.

"Yeah, it's OK. I like the Coke one, but they're always out of it."

"Ah man, that's the worst, right?"

"Yeah, I guess." Zack stabbed his straw into the slushee.

"Your name's Zack, right?"

"Uh... Yeah," Zack mumbled, suddenly suspicious. "Why?"

"Zack, what is the hold up? We have to get going..."

Sam didn't have to turn around to know the voice. He had heard it a thousand times in a thousand dreams in every corner of his psyche for the past eight years. It was sewn into his heart and into his ear drum, whatever was left of either. Sam turned around to face Lydia, who didn't even recognize him—until she did. Her face turned white. She was seeing a ghost. A real, honest to Jesus ghost of a life she had no inclination to revisit.

"Zack, go to the car," Lydia demanded, her voice shaking. Her cold eyes never left Sam's.

"I have to pay for my—"

"Put it down right now and go. GO."

"But you said-"

"Goddammit, Zack, go to the car!"

A befuddled Zack glanced at Sam and then back at his mom before setting his slushee down on the counter next to the machine. He shuffled out of the store, looking back one more time, confused. As soon as the jingle-jangle of the cowbell attached to the doors rang out, Lydia tore into Sam.

"What are you doing here?"

"Is he …?"

"You don't get to ask me questions."

"I'm not staying. I just—"

"What is this? What the fuck do you think this is?"

"I'm sorry, I just thought…"

"You don't get to come back here, Alan. Do you understand that?"

Sam's stunned silence ignited a fire inside of Lydia.

"DO YOU UNDERSTAND THAT?"

The outburst caught the attention of other store patrons. Sam lowered his voice, trying to diffuse Lydia's aggression.

"Can I just talk to you? For a minute? Somewhere? Please?" Lydia's eyes penetrated Sam's as her guard dropped briefly.

"I came all the way from Florida," Sam confessed. "I just want to say a few things. Some things I never had the chance to say."

"You had plenty of chances, Alan. You had a lifetime's worth of chances."

Sam's eyes found the floor. He had no defense. She was right.

The cowbell clanged again and Lydia's husband waddled into the store, searching for Lydia. But her eyes were trained on Sam.

"I'm not having this conversation in a Circle K," she whispered.

"Just give me half an hour," Sam pleaded. "You'll never see me again."

Lydia looked back at her husband who had somehow gotten lost in the tiny store. This bought her precious seconds. She turned back to Sam and whispered-

"Tomorrow morning. Denny's on the Beltway. Eight-thirty. If you're late, I'm gone."

Lydia's husband finally approached. "Everything okay, Liddy?" he asked, glancing briefly at Sam. Sam turned and made an impromptu white cherry slushee, promptly dropped it on the floor, and then loped out of the store like he had never existed.

"That guy say something to you?" Lydia's remarkably observant husband asked.

Lydia shook her head. "No, let's go."

CHAPTER 22

Loaded down by his few possessions and saddled with another hundred pounds of emotional baggage, Sam paraded through the streets of Cotton Mouth with no idea where he would go or what he would do for the next sixteen hours. And maybe that was for the best. He'd found Lydia and she'd granted him a chance to revisit their past. If nothing else came of this journey, that would be enough.

Weary and sweat-drenched, Sam stopped in a park and set his belongings down by a large Magnolia tree swirling with cicadas in the summer dusk. He collapsed against its trunk and tried to focus his thoughts, but they were flooding in too quickly for his brain to organize. He wondered if Cathy had made it out of Texas, or if the Monte Carlo had finally kicked the bucket somewhere in West Texas like Midland or Lubbock, where the land lays so flat you can see twenty miles in any direction. He retraced their journey and realized how relaxed he felt around her, emotionally and physically. How her skin felt warm and alive against his as she lay in the crook of his arm, her hair forever tinged with the smoke of Marlboro Reds.

Sam beheld the Magnolia tree and its strong, winding limbs stretching out toward the sky. Oversized, glossy green leaves wrapped and protected delicate white flowers like a coat from the cold. Sam thought about fatherhood and all of the years he had lost with Zack—if Zack was even his kid. But he had to be. Nothing else made sense. Sam thought about all of the things he had missed living in Florida and all of the things he wanted to make right if it wasn't too late. Sam wasn't a praying man, but as he sat underneath the shade of that giant tree, he hoped to God that it wasn't too late to turn this thing around.

Sam found his legs and went for a stroll through the park, past empty basketball courts, concrete bridges, and empty picnic benches. In the distance he could see a nearby farm-to-market road. Cars dashed back and forth every minute or so. In the other direction was a pauper's cemetery with crumbling, jagged tombstones plotted in no particular order. Sam thought about Ollie and how he would've liked to have known him. He still had no idea what had happened to him, but he couldn't help

251

feeling guilty for not having met Cathy a week sooner. Maybe he could've stopped it from happening, whatever it was. Maybe he could've been the father to Ollie that he wasn't to Zack. These thoughts only led him to sorrowful places. The sun was leaving for the day, so he figured he'd better find a place to sleep.

Sam splurged and spent eighty-nine dollars on a room at the finest hotel in town, the illustrious Cabanas at Cotton Mouth near the interstate. After checking in, he bought three candy bars from the vending machine, showered, changed the bandage on his stitched arm, cleaned the wax out of his busted ear drum, shaved his neck beard, laid his clothes out on the bed, turned on the TV, and fell asleep watching Hogan's Heroes.

#

Sam awoke sharply from an unsettling dream that evaporated the moment he reached consciousness. Vexed and disoriented, Sam found his bearings, rubbed his eyes and focused on an alarm clock that was blinking "12:00."

"Shit!" he yelled as he flew off the bed, sending candy bar wrappers onto the carpet below like a ticker-tape parade. He scooped up his watch on the dresser and pinned down the actual time, 8:12. "Fuck. Shit. Fuck!" The Denny's was at least a thirty-minute walk away. Sam threw his clothes on, gathered his shit and high-tailed it out of the room, leaving the TV on.

Sam made it to the Denny's in sixteen minutes, heaving a sigh of relief when he saw the sign. As his feet picked up steam again, he used the last block to center himself. Sam stopped at a crosswalk across the street from the restaurant and waited for the light to change from "Don't Walk" to "Walk." He flashed back to that Tallahassee intersection where a downtrodden Cathy stood alone with her guitar waiting for the same light to change. It was a street they had crossed together, but he had no one to hook arms with now. Sam scanned the Denny's parking lot and found Lydia's SUV parked near the front.

Sam slinked into the diner, which was packed with a rush of morning regulars. He peered out across a sea of tables, but didn't see Lydia anywhere. He glanced out the window to double check her car's presence. It was still there. She was here, somewhere.

"Alan?" a man's voice called from somewhere.

Sam turned toward a line of vinyl booths by the windows. There sat Lydia's husband, alone, waving him over. Sam slid past a waitress and approached the booth, exhausted, rattled and confused.

"I'm Lydia's husband, James," the man said.

"Where is Lydia?" Sam asked sternly.

253

"Please, have a seat," James said. Sam glared at James for a moment before reluctantly sitting. James slid a menu across the table to Sam. "The hash browns here are good."

Sam craned his neck toward the back of the restaurant. "Is she in the bathroom?"

James glared at the thick gauze wrapped around Sam's right arm. "What happened to your arm?" he asked.

"A window got in my way. Where is Lydia?"

James opened up the menu for Sam and flipped it to a page full of pancakes. "You should really try the pancakes here."

"I've been to fucking Denny's before," Sam snapped.

James leaned back in his booth and folded his fingers on the table in front of him. "She's not coming, Alan. I'm sorry."

Sam's face turned to concrete as he stared through James. "So she sent you."

James sipped his coffee and set it back down. "This is all too much for her, Alan. The way you showed up out of the blue."

A waitress came over and sat a plate with eggs, sausage, and hash browns in front of James. She slid a pad out of her smock and glared at Sam. "Can I get you something?"

"Nothing," Sam replied without making eye contact. Sam watched as James picked up a pepper shaker and maniacally dashed it on the potatoes. He debated his next move and realized he didn't have one. She wasn't here. She had sent her fucking husband. And now her fucking husband was peppering his potatoes. So much pepper. Sam began to wonder if James was going to use the whole shaker. He wondered what Lydia had seen in this man the first moment they met. Sam wasn't seeing it right now.

"How long have you been married?" Sam asked, finally breaking the silence.

James looked up from his hash browns and smiled proudly. "Six years."

Sam nodded, watching a family sitting two booths over.

"So the kid, he's …"

"Zack's my son," James insisted. "He's a great kid."

"Your son from a previous marriage, or…?"

The temperature in the booth dropped twenty degrees as James maniacally cut a sausage link into tiny pieces. He stuffed it into his mouth and stared at Sam with serious eyes. "Zack is my son with Lydia. Do you understand what I'm saying to you?"

Sam wasn't sure how to respond to the passive aggression coming out of the small, round man with a receding hair line ravenously stuffing scrambled egg into his mouth. Sam shook his head and stared out the window at the parking lot.

"I would've never left if I had known," Sam said.

James dropped his fork onto his plate and glared daggers at Sam. "If you had known what?"

"I would've stayed and tried to work things out with her, that's all I'm saying. I wasn't—I wasn't in the right state of mind. I wasn't acting like a husband. Christ, I should be saying these things to her, not you."

"What did you just say?"

"I said I wouldn't have left. I would've stayed."

"You didn't disappear, Alan. Lydia divorced you. It took six police officers to remove you from the house."

Sam's eyes narrowed. "Why would she have told you that?"

James polished off his eggs and started working on his hash browns. He glared up at Sam with a serious look in his eyes.

"She showed me the police report."

Sam's mind wandered through the hallways of his past, trying to piece together the truth. He had no recollection of these events. James cleaned his plate and took a giant gulp of water from a large plastic cup with no ice. He set it down on the table and wiped his mouth.

"So tell me, Alan. Why did you do it?" James inquired.

"Why did I do what?"

James leaned in, glanced left and right, then lowered his voice. "Why the hell'd you mow down those kids?"

James had lit a fuse in Sam. It was all that he could do to keep from exploding. He clenched his fists tightly under the table. "I fell asleep," Sam insisted. "It was an accident."

"Bullshit," James retorted, almost smiling. "The next door neighbor said he saw you plow into those kids wide-eyed and fully awake."

"THAT'S A LIE!" Sam yelled, slamming his fist down on the table as cups flew and dishes clanked. The Denny's fell silent. All eyes were on them now. Overwhelmed by it all, Sam jerked up from the booth.

"This was a bad idea," he said to James, who remained seated, staring.

"You're damn right it was," James said. He scooted his fat ass out of the booth and followed Sam into the parking lot.

"You stay away from my family, asshole!" James yelled. "You hear me?!"

Sam walked quickly toward the edge of the parking lot but James wasn't satisfied. "You don't belong anywhere, Alan! You're a ghost!"

Sam stopped at the curb and whipped around, rage alive in his eyes. "Give me my Willie Nelson record," he asserted with quiet insanity.

"What?"

"You picked it up yesterday in your driveway. It belongs to me."

James burned an even darker shade of red. "You were at my house?"

Sam paced quickly toward the SUV. He peered into the front passenger window.

"There it is. Give it to me."

"Get away from my car!" James said, rushing toward Sam as he pried open the passenger door and wrangled the record off the floorboard. James grabbed Sam and attempted to steal the record back, and a tussle ensued. Despite Sam's injured arm flopping uselessly at his side and his good arm clutching the record, he put up a valiant fight.

"Let go of it!" Sam exclaimed. "My grandfather gave it to me!" Sam attempted to peel James' fingers off the record.

"Get your hands off me!" James barked, sending a flying elbow that landed squarely on Sam's nose. Sam fell backwards to the asphalt, landing on top of his already damaged arm. He cried out in pain, his nose dripping blood onto Willie Nelson's face. Sam peeled himself up from the parking lot. "I hope my son doesn't grow up to be an asshole like his dad," Sam blurted.

"I'm confused. In this fantasy, are you referring to me or yourself?"

"Fuck you, James!"

The Denny's waitress ran out of the restaurant toward James. "Sir, you have to pay for your food," she scowled.

Sam stepped off the parking lot curb into the street as the red light behind him turned green and traffic began to zoom past. "You'll never see me again," Sam stated calmly, his mouth and chin covered in his own blood. Sam turned around and drifted into the hectic street as cars honked and weaved to avoid him.

James' eyes grew silver-dollar wide as he watched the ghost cross the tightrope. Sam somehow made it to the other side unscathed, and he kept marching, his record in hand. James looked down at his Denny's receipt, then handed a twenty dollar bill to the waitress.

#

Sam's feet seemed to instinctively know the direction to the nearest bus station, even if he didn't. They propelled him forward, one foot in front of the other down the smoldering Texas blacktop as the sun worked its way ever closer to its noontime peak. Fuck, was it hot—so blazing that the sun had already dried the blood that had cascaded from his nose onto his shoulder and his shirt. The bleeding had stopped but Sam's arm hurt like hell, and his ego was equally bruised. Sam briefly considered returning to his brother's house and beating the crap out of him, but it would be a pointless act. There was no water left in that

259

well. He should've cut ties fifteen years ago when his parents died, but he hadn't. As the more responsible of the two, he'd carried the reins as long as he could. Be he wasn't his father. Not even close. And he never should've trusted his brother with money. He knew better.

A western wear store loomed up around the curve. Sam knew no sensible bus driver would allow him to board with his current look, which could best be described as injured boxer meets sunburned zombie. Through the store's window Sam saw a mannequin in full regalia—boots, jeans, pressed pearl snap shirt, and cowboy hat. Simultaneously, Sam saw his disheveled, blood-stained, road-weary reflection in the plate glass. Sam reached into his shirt pocket and discovered the cash that Cathy had given him. Ten minutes and a few odd looks later, he exited the store wearing the outfit from mannequin, save for the shirt, which was swapped out for a solid denim version, Sam's trade-mark.

Sam reached the Greyhound parking lot just in time to see one of the silver eagles roll out of the parking lot en route to Oklahoma City. Inside the station, a handful of lost souls loi-tered and waited for their rides. Two large LCD screens above an archway displayed cities and times. Sam had his pick of desti-nations, and a highlighted bus to Los Angeles leaving in two hours caught his eye. He wondered what Cathy would say if he actually showed up.

Sam approached the ticket counter, which was manned by a small, overworked woman with a nametag that read "Angel." She looked up with the kind of tired eyes that only double shifts can produce.

"Where to?" she asked, smacking a piece of yesterday's gum.

"Los Angeles," Sam said. "The four o'clock bus."

Angel pressed a variety of buttons on her computer. "You're in luck," she said. We have one seat left on that bus." Sam realized in that moment that this was meant to happen.

"How much?" he asked, then immediately said, "it doesn't matter. I'll take it."

Angel nodded blankly. "I still have to tell you how much it is so you can pay me, is that okay?"

"That'd be great."

"Eighty-five seventy-five, with tax."

Sam pulled out his remaining wad of cash and laid a $100 bill on the counter. "Keep the change," he said. He instantly felt his hands and legs tingle, and somewhere deep inside he began to feel reborn, as though the road had changed him. He felt like he was making his first right decision in a decade filled with lost maps and broken roads. Angel checked the bill with a counterfeit pen, verified its authenticity, and then stuck it in her cash drawer. A machine clanked and printed a boarding ticket, which Angel slid across the counter along with $14.25 in change.

"We're not allowed to take tips," she said.

Sam sat in the lobby for the next hour with his bonsai tree occupying the seat next to him while his bag and records laid at his feet. Sam glanced at the back of his bus ticket and read the words "non-refundable," then looked down at his bandage and noticed blood seeping through. Terrified for a moment, the surgeon inside of him kicked in and he carried his sleeping bag into the bathroom and locked himself in the cleanest stall he could find. Sam sat on the toilet and slowly unwrapped the gauze from his arm to discover that four of his sixteen stitches had been yanked out during his altercation with James. The blood seeped out of his forearm in pulses, dark, almost black. Sam opened his sleeping bag and pulled out his first aid kit. The bottle of rubbing alcohol was empty—he'd used it all on that son of a bitch cowboy. Sam accepted that he was going to have to do this without antiseptic, and it was going to hurt like a mother fucker. He retrieved his thread and a spare needle, and then, with a sharp wince and squeeze of his eyelids, he began to stitch up his arm as the blood continued to dripped out.

Sam released a deep breath as he walked out of the Greyhound bathroom, his arm stitched up with fifteen minutes left before his bus arrived. As he returned to his seat, Angel the ticket seller made a bee line for him.

"Your bus broke down in El Paso," Angel said.

"Oh," Sam replied.

"It'll be here. It's going to be late."

"How late?"

"They said seven o'clock. That's the best case scenario. It could be nine or ten."

Sam nodded. "Okay. I guess I'll just wait then."

"There's a Church's Chicken about two blocks from here, if you get hungry or something."

Sam sat up in his seat. "Thanks, that's a good tip."

Angel agreed and slunk back to her ticket booth, where someone was already waiting for her.

#

Sam sat for another hour, but his nerves were shot from the stitches and his feet wouldn't keep still—his whole body wanted to keep moving. With at least two hours to kill and his mind racing, Sam departed the friendly, air-conditioned confines and set out on a walk— a farewell jaunt in the state that had birthed him, spit him out, and reeled him back in. As he headed north on foot, way past the Church's Chicken, Sam became disoriented. He wasn't lost—he knew these roads—but for some reason, he couldn't find his bearings.

Sam kept roaming. After he passed by a Waffle House and a newly-constructed gas station, the traffic thinned and cars stopped whizzing by at such a steady clip. The landscape grew more and more rural the further he walked, and Sam suddenly recognized that he was on his old route home. He stopped briefly and considered the highway, then turned back around again and adjusted his new cowboy hat. The stretch in the road pushed uphill over a sharp curve in the distance. Sam's heart rate jumped as he reached the blind curve at the top of the hill. He had arrived.

Sam stared at a modest, ranch-style home on the left side of the road. He scrutinized the asphalt and discovered faint tire marks. A pair of cars whooshed by close to where he stood on the shoulder, almost spinning him around. His legs carried him up the gravel shoulder until he reached a black mail box with the name "Campbell" spelled out in reflective silver stickers.

Sam stared up a long, winding sidewalk past two hedges and a lamp post. That's where the woman had stood, screaming. Where she had peered helplessly into the yard, where the boys lay dying. There was nothing there now but patchy grass and a few stubborn weeds. Sam didn't welcome the images that were rushing back into his head like old 8mm movies, but he would not avoid them any longer. He still couldn't remember what happened—only the aftermath.

Sam stood there for ten minutes in a trance before the front door of the ranch house popped open. Sam glanced up—and there stood the woman, eight years older, staring back at him. It was like some sort of dream, but it wasn't. He was awake and standing in her yard. He had no idea if she recognized him, but he had to say something, he supposed.

"I'm sorry," Sam said. "I think I got lost."

"Do you need to use a phone?" the woman asked.

"I don't believe so."

"Please, come inside," the woman said, then turned and disappeared into the house. Sam stood between the hedges without a clue. He stared back at the street, then gazed at the wide open front door.

#

Sam took off his hat and sat down on a large leather sofa in a living room with vaulted ceilings. The house was cold, too cold, even for summer. He glared up at pair of recessed lights in the ceiling that seemed to shine on him directly like spotlights. He glanced down as the woman appeared from the kitchen with a Mason jar full of iced tea.

"Have something to drink," she said, offering the jar to Sam. He took it gratefully, adopting an automatic southern drawl he hadn't used since his teen years. "Thank you, ma'am."

265

Sam lifted the glass and felt the ridges of the jar slip between his lips as he took a long, refreshing sip, nearly finishing the glass in one gulp. The woman sat down on the couch right next to him, too close for comfort.

"You have a lovely home," Sam said, her close proximity clearly making him uneasy.

"What did you do to your arm?" the woman asked.

"I cut it," Sam said. "It was an accident."

"I'm sorry to hear that you were in an accident," the woman said. "You should be more careful."

A long silence followed. Sam could feel the woman staring at him. He took another long, nervous sip of tea, finishing the glass. He set it down gently on the coffee table in front of him, then quickly looked back at the woman before shifting his eyes to a distant wall. He could hear the air conditioner cut on in the hallway, and soon more frigid air flowed through vents overhead.

"You can stop wondering," the woman finally said. "I know who you are. And I know why you're here."

Sam's heart raced. For the first time, he truly looked at her. She had a nose and lips and two ears and a mouth, but there was nothing behind her hollow, brown eyes but sorrow.

"I don't know what to say," Sam said.

"You don't have to say anything," she replied. "Just sit here and let me look at you."

Sam complied. He felt like a nude model in a college art class. As odd as the request was, Sam figured he owed it to her. Sam's eyes searched the room and eventually landed on a photo of the woman with a man, in happier times.

"Will your husband be home soon?" he asked.

"I doubt it. He left three years ago."

Sam lowered his head. "I'm sorry."

"We held on as long as we could," the woman said. "Some things, you can't keep forever. They just don't stay."

Sam considered the woman's comments. An eternity passed. Sam looked at the woman once again, then stared at the carpet.

"I think about what happened," he admitted. "It lives inside me. It's always there. It changed me. I lost something, but it was nothing compared to what I took from you. I wish I could remember what happened, and I wish I knew why."

The woman guided her hand over to Alan's chin and turned his face toward hers.

"You fell asleep, Alan. That's it."

The words landed in the middle of Sam's chest. How could this woman be so calm, so welcoming, so forgiving, when he hadn't even begun to forgive himself?

267

"Do you hate me?" he asked, trembling, unsure if he really wanted to know the answer. The woman slid over a couple of inches on the couch and placed her hand on top of his. It felt cold and warm at the same time. Her bony fingers slid into his and began to squeeze. Sam looked up at the woman and felt as though she could see all the way through him to the other side of the couch. He was paralyzed, physically, emotionally, and psychologically.

"Not anymore," she said, her grip growing more intense. Sam wanted to cry, to let go of everything that had built up over the last decade, to release all of the energy that had been controlling him, sending him weaving into oncoming traffic. But Sam didn't cry. He let out a long, slow breath and felt the woman's fingers slide out of his own. He stared ahead at a wall covered in memories—the woman's whole life on display—and here he was, the man who had taken it all away.

"Are you okay?" she asked.

"I was just thinking about a dream that I had last night."

"Tell me about it."

Sam cleared his throat. "I was married and living in this house, a two-story, except I didn't recognize the street. It was a different street, right in the middle of the block. It was Christmastime and the whole family was there, mine and hers, and all the lights in the neighborhood were filling up the night sky with white and red and green. I went outside for some reason. I put on my coat. I expected it to be cold, but it wasn't—it was muggy and warm, and I looked through a large window at the corner of the house and I could see my family sitting around the dining table, laughing and enjoying food and drinks and conversation. There was a noise. I turned back toward the street. Two houses down, across the street, I could see it... falling silently. An airplane, a commercial jet, maybe a 747, barreling downward. A hundred miles an hour. And it made no noise at all, even at impact. But there was a ball of fire and I was thrown back into the bushes, and when I got up, I couldn't hear anything. I was deaf. But I could see that my house was on fire. I scrambled to my feet and ran back to the window but I didn't see my family. They were gone. I grabbed a garden hose and carried it over to the corner of the house where the fire was, and I sprayed as hard as I could, but the jet fuel was too much. As the flames engulfed the house, I backed out into the street, hose still in hand, and the whole thing just lit up, all the trees, everything. The heat was so intense, I thought my face was going to melt. I couldn't even keep my eyes open. I felt something touch my foot, and when I looked down there was an empty airplane seat next to me. Then I woke up."

The woman stared at Sam. She appeared lost as she eyed the empty mason jar on the table in front of him. "Let me get you a refill," she said.

"That's okay," Sam said. "I should probably be going."

"Please, stay. Let me get you some more iced tea."

Sam acquiesced, and watched as the woman stepped around the couch and into the kitchen. He heard a refrigerator door open, ice dispense from a machine, liquid hitting glass, and then quiet. Sam's eyes trained on one of the photos on the wall—her two boys. It was the first time he had seen him with their eyes open.

Sam glanced up and discovered the woman standing in the kitchen entrance completely naked, holding a glass of iced tea. She was nervous, shaking slightly.

"If you'd like to have this tea, it will be in my bedroom with me," she said, taking a small sip. Before Sam could respond, she slowly turned and walked down a long, carpeted hallway. She disappeared into her bedroom, and the house fell silent.

Sam sat immobile, completely off guard. He looked back at the photo of the two boys he had killed. Suddenly, a cuckoo clock in the living room came alive and bellowed seven distinct coos, signaling the seven o'clock hour.

"Shit."

Sam flew out of the house in a full sprint until his feet hit the fiery asphalt. He arrived at the Greyhound station twenty minutes later, just in time to see the bus to Los Angeles chug out of the parking lot and rumble up the Interstate 10 entrance ramp. Sam gave chase and attempted to flag the driver down, but the bus had a destiny that didn't include him. Sam collapsed in a heap in the corner of the Greyhound parking lot, his clothes completely covered in sweat and his bandage dangerously close to slipping off again.

Sam cursed as he bent over and retrieved his scuffed cowboy hat from the parking lot. He glanced back at the bus station as his breath slowly returned, then slogged across the scorching gravel toward the building.

"I missed my bus," Sam said to Angel, stating the obvious.

"You sure did," she replied.

"When's the next bus to Los Angeles?"

Angel pressed a few buttons on her computer before delivering the fatal news.

"Monday."

Sam slumped, then heard the squeal of air brakes behind him. He turned around to see another bus pulling into the lot.

"Where's that one going?" he asked desperately. Angel checked the schedule on her computer.

"Florida."

271

Of course it was.

Sam glared at the bus, then back at Angel. "How much?" he asked.

Angel smiled. "Forty dollars."

CHAPTER 23

Cathy made it halfway across the desolate, arrow-straight West Texas plains before the Monte Carlo started acting up. After a couple of jump starts in Midland and Odessa, the damn thing finally broke down for good as Cathy sputtered into Gallup, New Mexico around eleven p.m. Cathy found herself stranded and alone along a pitch black stretch of Interstate 40. In the distance, beautiful vistas lived under the cover of darkness. Cathy couldn't see them, but she could feel their presence.

Cathy popped the hood and cursed the engine. She retrieved a bottle of coolant from the passenger seat and desperately poured the last of it into the engine, using her dying cell phone as a flashlight. An eighteen-wheeler roared past, blinding her and blowing her back, but she remained steadfast. She re-

273

turned to the car and attempted to crank the engine. It responded with three clicks.

"Come on girl, one more time, please," Cathy pleaded. She tried it again. Again, three clicks. Cathy slammed her palms against the steering wheel until the base of her hands began to bleed, then sat in the dark and stared out the windshield. Perhaps this was the end of the road.

Just as the ache in her hands finally hit her, a pair of white lights pulled up behind her. Cathy was relieved to discover a trucker pulling over to help. After attempting a jump start—which failed—he offered to give Cathy a ride to a nearby truck stop. She graciously accepted, despite the fact that she would be entering a stranger's cab in the middle of the night in the middle of nowhere. Cathy dove into the backseat of the Monte Carlo and retrieved her bag and the guitar case containing her money. She spied Sam's guitar in the backseat, but didn't have hands to carry it, so she covered it with a t-shirt. Then she hopped in the eighteen-wheeler, as the hydraulic rush of air brakes filled her ears.

After a half hour of monotonous, sleep-inducing small talk, Cathy was relieved to see the shining lights of a Lucky Lady truck stop on the horizon. Cathy thanked the trucker, grabbed her belongings and hopped out, making a bee line for the diner inside. Cathy entered and found the smoke-filled café filled to the brim with the usual clientele. Despite the madness, she managed to score a corner booth, sliding in mere seconds before a waiter arrived with the obligatory cup of coffee.

"Thank you," Cathy said, looking up.

"You eating?"

"I think this'll be it for now," Cathy responded. The gum-smacking waitress moved on to the next one, and Cathy let go of a long-held breath. There was plenty to stress about, but for now, Cathy just sipped from her steaming cup of coffee and enjoyed the comfort of air conditioning for the first time in forty-eight hours. She didn't know what the hell she was going to do about her car, but it would have to wait until morning. Cathy slid her hand along the top of the guitar case next to her. The texture immediately felt wrong. "No, no, no," she said urgently as she snapped open the guitar's clasps. She peeked inside, terrified to find exactly what she was about to find.

Sam's guitar.

Her money—her lifeline, nine thousand dollars in cash—was sitting in an unguarded, dusty guitar case in an abandoned car on the side of the highway, a Jimmy Buffett "Margaritaville" t-shirt the only protection it had from prying eyes. And apart from traipsing twenty-three miles back on foot, there wasn't a fucking thing Cathy could do about it right now.

275

Cathy sat speechless, her appetite gone. She considered her next plan of action. There was no safe way back to the car tonight, that was a given. She decided she would stay at the diner until morning and try to catch a ride back to her car then. In the meantime, she would cross her fingers and hope that it wasn't touched overnight. Cathy reached into her jeans pocket and counted the cash she had on her: a whopping sixty dollars. She shook her head. That wouldn't get her to California, but she was savvy. She would get there one way or another. There was no other option.

Cathy knew she should find a place to sleep, but it wasn't going to happen tonight, not with the fear of the unknown hanging over her head. So she sat there, hogging the corner booth from one a.m. until sunrise, watching countless truckers file in, eat, and leave. Delirium set in around four o'clock as Cathy found herself counting the kitchen tiles that she could see from the dining room.

The sun was barely above the horizon when Cathy caught a ride back to her car with a soft-spoken lady trucker named Pamela. The drive took thirty minutes but the silence in the cab mixed with the anticipation for what awaited made it feel like ten years to Cathy. As the Monte Carlo mercifully appeared in the distance, Cathy's nerves took over.

"Is that it?" Pamela asked.

"Yes," Cathy responded, almost shaking, her eyes trained on the car that inched ever closer. Those breathtaking vistas, now kissed by the rising eastern sun, remained unseen by Cathy, who was hyper focused on her car.

The semi came to a noisy halt behind the car. "This'll just take a minute," Cathy said, staring out the windshield.

"Take your time," Pamela responded. Cathy climbed out of the big rig and slowly approached the car. Through the back windshield she could see the Jimmy Buffett t-shirt draped across the case, a good sign. As she reached the car, a semi whipped by at 90 miles per hour, its wind almost knocking Cathy off her feet. She regained her balance and opened the door. The crisp New Mexico wind took hold of it, breaking the hinge and pinning it back against the car's front quarter panel. It was as if the Monte Carlo was self-destructing along with Cathy.

Cathy climbed inside and snatched up the Jimmy Buffett t-shirt. She caressed the guitar case that lay underneath, a long lost friend, a savior. Cathy breathed a quick sigh of relief before bravely unlatching the case and lifting the lid.

There was no guitar in that case.

There was no money in that case.

All that remained was the case, a cheap, rotting, manufactured piece of chipboard. The world was ending.

Cathy emerged from the car with the case, a zombie. She moved back towards Pamela's truck, wavering dangerously closer to the highway with each step she took.

#

"There's a bus stop about three miles from here," Pamela said as she steered her rig down the interstate with Cathy back in the passenger seat.

"That sounds fine, thank you," Cathy muttered, her face turned to stone.

"Hell, I could take you all the way to Reno if you're going further west."

Pamela looked over at Cathy who gripped the guitar case tight against her chest, her arms wrapped around it like she was cradling a child. In many ways, she was. Lost deep in her own psyche, Cathy stared blankly out the windshield as the unending white lines on the interstate flew past.

"You okay, lady?" Pamela asked, spying Cathy's guitar case. "That must be one important guitar."

Cathy glared at the stocky woman with the buzz cut and flannel shirt who was prying into her life.

"You on the road a lot?" Cathy asked.

"Oh yeah," Pamela said. "This is my job."

Cathy stared out the windshield as the white lines kept on coming with no end in sight.

278

"It must be hard, having no one," Cathy said. "Being alone. Having no family. No one to go home to. You must spend a lot of time thinking about the things you did that kept you alone. It must feel lonely, spending your life without anyone."

Pamela looked over at Cathy, confused, hurt, at a loss for words, if only temporarily.

Five minutes later the air brakes engaged and the semi rolled into a Greyhound bus station just off the highway.

"Thank you for the ride," Cathy said after Pamela opened up the passenger door. Before Cathy could slide out of her seat, Pamela touched her shoulder.

"I don't know you, young lady, but I'd like you to know something about me. I'm forty six years old, and I'm married to a beautiful lady. We have two beautiful daughters and one ugly dog. The only thing that keeps me on this road is the thought of their faces when I come home, and the only things I think about are the good times I spend with them. With my family. And I believe they call that love. I hope you have that in your life somewhere, and if not, then I hope you find it someday."

Cathy stared down at the latches on her guitar case and nodded silently.

"I should be going now."

With that, Cathy escaped the truck and found the warm New Mexico pavement.

CHAPTER 24

Sam spent his thirty-six hour ride back to Florida staring out of a tinted window at the same sights he had seen on the way to Texas—this time from the opposite side of the highway. Sam found it humorous and humbling to discover that he could see the same things for the first time again. He tried to get a better sense of the world as it flew by him again. As the Greyhound rolled through Shreveport, past the glittery neon of the casinos, Sam thought about Cathy and wondered where he might be if he had made it back in time to catch that bus to California. Sam sunk down into his cracked vinyl seat and attempted to sleep, but the three-hundred-pound Samoan man next to him occupied about half of his space. Sam pinned his forehead against the warm glass and let the sun flicker on his face, but he didn't close his eyes.

Giving up on sleep, Sam reached down and picked up one of his records, Jerry Jeff Walker's *Ridin' High*. Its worn, water-stained cover featured a photo of a cowboy in his early forties atop a sturdy colt, his smiling eyes penetrating the camera and his right hand gently gripping the brim of a well-worn cowboy hat. Behind him, a dusty grey sky went on for miles. Sam pinched open the cardboard cover and pulled out the record sleeve. As a lyric sheet slipped loose from the cover, Sam felt something glance against the top of his foot. Sam fished around his ankles with his face dangerously close to the sleeping Samoan's crotch. On the floor he found a yellowed, folded piece of notebook paper. Sam could see cursive ink through the folds. He gently opened it. It was a letter dated August 4, 1969. The penmanship was graceful, delicate, and flowed with ease. It began *"Dear Ray,"*

Sam immediately realized it was written to his grandfather. The letter continued:

"You are the love of my life. I don't know why the sky opened up and dropped you into my world, and I don't know why it waited so long to do so. I am confident that the love in my heart would fill three lifetimes, if only it could pump enough blood. This time belongs to us, but it also belongs to another. June has found July, and we are stars that shine in separate skies. I feel no shame, but I am broken. I will always be broken. My love remains, Virginia."

Sam stared at the letter. His grandfather had married his grandmother when he had returned from World War II, but her name wasn't Virginia. It was June. Sam folded the letter and stuck it back in the record sleeve, where it had lived for so many years, untouched and unread, then stared out of the bus window at the highway blurring past.

#

The Greyhound rolled into Tampa the next afternoon at three o'clock in the afternoon. Before getting off the bus, Sam decided to leave his Jerry Jeff Walker and blood-stained Willie Nelson album behind for someone else to discover. He slid them under his seat next to the Samoan.

Sam stepped off the bus with his sleeping bag, bonsai tree and John Prine record, completely unprepared for the all-consuming wall of humidity that welcomed him back to the great state of Florida. He ambled toward the bus station, but stopped short when he realized he couldn't fathom another bus ride, not even one as short as sixty miles. Instead, Sam hired a taxi to take him back to Escapade, a ninety-minute ride that cost him twice as much as the bus that had carried him from Texas. He had a little bit of Cathy's money left to burn, and he felt wrong holding on to any of it.

Per Sam's request, the taxi dropped him off in the middle of downtown Escapade. Sam made a bee line for Jones Diner, where he promptly ordered chicken-fried steak and devoured it like he hadn't eaten in a month. People stared at him as he gorged, but for once he didn't mind feeling like one of the tourists.

After he finished eating, Sam huffed it up the long, steep hill toward the cemetery he knew so well. His legs were jelly by the time he reached the sprawling iron gates of Memorial Cemetery. Before entering, he decided to trek across the street to Dan's Grave Markers. He stayed along the perimeter of the street and marched around to the backyard, where he peeked through a hole in the privacy fence. There he saw a new guy, shorter than Sam, but more clean cut. Definitely younger. He sand-blasted a stone while another fresh hire, an older fellow—a white Maurice—fired up the diamond saw on the other side of the yard. Sam smiled. Things were as they should be. The machine hadn't changed, only the cogs within it. Sam glanced down at his sleeping bag and spotted one of his engraving tools poking out of the side. He had carried them all the way to Texas and back for no explainable reason. He peered back toward the cemetery. Suddenly, the reason hit him.

Sam weaved through headstones until he spotted a familiar oak tree with wild, reaching limbs and all the shade anyone could ever ask for. Just past it, the stone read "Ollie Triumph. April 5, 2013—June 1, 2015. The Angels are singing." Sam ap-

283

proached slowly, examining his handiwork. He moved closer and slid his hand across the jagged and uneven pearly gate graphic at the top. Sam pulled the chisel and mallet from his sleeping bag, and with the sun beginning to set through the tree line, he methodically etched and smoothed out the pearly gate graphic. At first, the tools felt foreign in his hands, but only for a moment, until it all came back to him.

Everything came back to him.

By the time he finished, the sun had long since set. He stepped back and took one last look at Ollie's gravestone, lit only by the light of the Florida moon. "Sorry it took me so long," Sam said to no one and to everyone. He placed his tools on the ground and then picked up his well-traveled bonsai tree from the ground. He pulled a half-empty bottle of water from his bag and poured it onto the plant, filling it to its edges, then he carried it to Ollie's tombstone and placed it on top.

"This is where you belong," Sam said.

#

Four-thousand miles away, Cathy reached Los Angeles in a green 2004 Nissan Sentra with air conditioning. Within two hours, she had checked into a motel and written the following song lyrics, which she had carried inside her head on the road without writing them down.

Drivin' down this long and lonesome highway

284

Headlight's been burned out for three damn days
If summer's ghost comes floatin' around that curve
I don't think I'll have the nerve to move
I left a lot of blood out on that dance floor
When I close my eyes I see you standing there
I'll force that smile with a cigarette in hand
We never had a plan, it's true, and you...
When you run, well I hope your legs don't move
I wish that I could hold on to the things I hold on to
When you run from something you never knew
Where will I be?

#

As Sam tramped a familiar path through the streets of Escapade, he counted the number of boats parked in between houses for old time's sake. By the time he reached seventy-four, he had arrived at a street he never imagined he would see again: Sunswept Drive. The neighborhood was a ghost town. As he reached the barricades, he noticed something odd—a fucking miracle, actually.

His house was still standing.

Sam jogged through a dozen different scenarios, but the only one that made sense was confirmed by the demolition note still plastered to the front door. "Demolition scheduled for July 1," the note read. Sam squinted at his wristwatch, barely lit by the moon. The tiny windows inside its face read "TUES" and "30."

"Holy shit," Sam said, glancing back up at the notice. "That's tomorrow." Sam had somehow made it back home in time to say goodbye.

An uneasy feeling overcame him. He turned around and discovered that the sinkhole that had once stopped at the edge of his neighbor's curb had now swallowed ten feet of his own yard. Every instinct told him to leave, to get the hell out of there. Naturally, Sam turned back around, pulled out his keys, stuck them in the front door lock, and walked inside.

Sam walked into a space he barely recognized. Everything was as he had left it, but it all seemed so different, like it belonged to someone else. Like it wasn't ever his to begin with. Sam stepped into the pitch black living room and plopped down on his sofa. He spotted his television remote control in front of him on the coffee table. He scooped it up and pressed "on," as if that would miraculously restore the electricity that had been cut off weeks ago. It didn't. Sam sat alone in the dark for several minutes, staring at the blank TV. He used to sit in this same spot and watch headlights from passing cars streak across the wall, but there were none to be found this evening. Sam stood up and walked into the kitchen, where he unwisely opened the fridge and became consumed by the smell of rotten everything.

286

It filled his nose and throat and made him cough almost to the point of vomiting, but he somehow held it at bay as he shut the door.

Sam stumbled to the back door and flung it open in an attempt to let in some fresh air. He stepped out and took a long, curious look into his backyard, now overgrown with grass and weeds up to his waist.

"I'll be a son of a bitch," he declared, unable to contain his smile.

In the middle of the yard, his long suffering disappointment of a banana tree stood tall and proud, overflowing with ripe bananas. Sam couldn't believe it. He plodded up to the tree, picked a banana off of it and peeled it back to take a bite. Satisfied, he held the peel up toward the tree. "It's about time, buddy."

Sam retreated back into the house, leaving the patio door open. He finished the banana and dropped the peel in the living room before roaming into his bedroom. He stared at his bed with heavy eyes. The covers were pulled back, just as he had left them. Sam thought about lying down, but he feared he might fall asleep the moment he did. He stood in the dark, listening to the silence of the newly deserted neighborhood. It had never been this fucking quiet.

Sam laid his sleeping bag down on the carpet next to the bed and carefully propped the John Prine record up against it. He sat down on the bed, feeling the familiar spring of his old mattress welcoming him back. He laid his head back on his pillow and stared up at the ceiling. Just for a few moments, he thought. He closed his eyes. It was 12:23 a.m.

#

Two hours later in a dive bar in Glendale, California, Cathy stepped on stage in front of nine people with Sam's guitar strapped around her neck. She had no nerves—just a head full of songs and a heart full of wandering hope. She gazed out at the scant crowd. Most of them were drinking and socializing. She keyed in on one young college-aged girl sitting alone and nursing a Long Island Iced Tea. She was the only one paying attention.

"This is a song I wrote for a friend of mine," Cathy said into a worn microphone. "It's called *Disguise*." She made eye contact with the young girl in the bar. "This one's for you Sam Stone, wherever you are."

Cathy adjusted her guitar strap then began to strum an alternating chord pattern. When she opened her mouth to sing her voice rang out strong and true, and somewhere deep inside she believed that Sam could hear her.

Do you feel that rain on your face?
You've been waiting.

In the vacant, haunting quiet of Sunswept Drive, dirt began to quickly recede and crumble from the edges of the sinkhole that bordered Sam's house.

For a brand new start. And brand new eyes.
I'll see you.

The earth whooshed down in large chunks as mounds of grass began to collapse.

The sinkhole widened with thundering force, reaching Sam's front door in a matter of seconds. Inside, Sam lay fast asleep on his bed.

Down every road, in every song, we used to sing.

The roaring sinkhole consumed the living room, sucking Sam's couch and TV into oblivion before splitting left and right toward the kitchen and hall simultaneously. In the bedroom, Sam awoke, disoriented, as the fury of the sinkhole shook his entire house. His eyes filled with fear as he realized where he was and what was happening.

289

But I'll take this time, wearing this disguise.
Waiting for some light to shine my way.

Sam careened off the bed and landed on his stomach on the floor. He could hear the sinkhole thundering through the hallway toward him like a freight train, disintegrating everything in its path.

So don't think twice. It's wrong. It's right.
It's here, then it's gone, gone away.

Sam clenched his eyes tight and gripped his bed post as nature's unforgiving fury barreled into his room. His only possible escape route was the window, which might as well have been a mile away. But there was no time. The earth had come for him.

In moments like these, seconds before death, it's been said that life flashes before a person's eyes. This was not true for Sam Stone. There was no slow-motion ending. No memories came flooding back. There was only quick, cold, black soil, and the sudden loss of gravity. In a suffocating free fall of dirt, Sam's world suddenly went black.

And a heart won't be the only thing that breaks.

No a heart won't be the only thing that breaks.

#

Cathy escaped the smoky confines of the bar around 1 a.m. and set out on foot down a stretch of well-worn sidewalk on a balmy Los Angeles night. Cathy looked up at bugs swarming streetlamps underneath arching, fifty-foot tall palm trees, and she suddenly felt like the smallest creature in the world. She also felt alone. She settled in on a bus bench and could vaguely make out the vacant shadows of Griffith Park in the distance. She realized in that moment that her heart was still beating in her chest, and that the headlights approaching in the distance belonged to the bus that would take her somewhere else.

Cathy climbed onto the bus and sat down across from its only other passengers, a Hispanic woman in her 20's and her two-year-old son. As the bus swayed and dipped, Cathy eyed the pair, the taste of tequila still alive on her tongue.

"Little late to have a child out, isn't it?" Cathy asked the woman. The woman looked up, confused, but she soon realized that Cathy could only be talking to her.

"How old is he?" Cathy asked.

The woman half smiled. "Sorry. No speak a English."

"Oh, that's okay," Cathy replied, and then the bus sat silent for the next two minutes as Cathy continued to stare at the little boy. Something was growing inside of her, and it would soon

291

move from the pit of her stomach, find her throat and escape out of her mouth.

"I had a son," Cathy said suddenly. "About his age."

The woman smiled, no clue as to what Cathy was saying.

"I had just started this new job. I've had a lot of jobs. Mostly shitty jobs. I couldn't afford a day care center. So I found this lady online... Ms. Renee. She ran a day care out of her house. It wasn't licensed, but it was eighty dollars a week. I didn't want to put Ollie in day care at all, but my ex—Ollie's dad—he wasn't in the picture. He didn't even know he had a son. My work had been messing with my hours a lot, days one week, nights the next. Well they called me in to work a morning shift about two hours after my night shift ended. I was dead on my feet, but what are you gonna do?"

The woman nodded, feigning comprehension as Cathy shifted in her seat.

"I was barely hanging on, just exhausted. I got Ollie out of bed, got him dressed, fed him something, I don't know what. Got him in his car seat and we headed to Ms. Renee's. I remember he fell asleep on the way. He never did that. So, Ms. Renee's, then I went to work at nine o'clock."

Cathy paused, something hitting her. Her voice changed.

"It must've been two... I took an early lunch so I walked out to go next door to the 7/11, and there was a commotion in the parking lot. People were crying, and I looked and I saw that they were around my car. I ran over and that's when I saw..."

The interior lights in the bus flickered as it rolled over a bump. The strobe affect gave an eerie glow to the tears that began to stream out of Cathy's eyes.

"They had pulled him out of the car, total strangers. They had broken a window and they had laid him on the... on the parking lot... And he wasn't... He wasn't there. He was already gone. And his little eyes..."

Cathy sobbed.

"His little eyes were open. And his mouth. So dry. His little tongue. I could see. He fought for it. For air. Until he couldn't fight any more."

The tears were coming in droves now and Cathy somehow began to shiver on an impossibly hot, stifling bus.

"And the police came, and the ambulance, and there was nothing anyone could do. It was too late. And I told the officer, I told him what happened. That I dropped him off at Ms. Renee's and then went to work. I told him that. And he put his hand on my shoulder and he looked at me and said, "These things happen every day, ma'am."

Cathy sucked in as much air as she could, she was hyperventilating now. The woman stared in shock, clutching her son.

Cathy closed her eyes. "But what I didn't tell him... What I couldn't tell him... was that I knew. I went in to work and I knew that he was still in there. I put on my shirt and I served drinks and I dispensed tokens and I knew. I knew, and I did nothing, and I don't know why."

Cathy opened her eyes, glaring at the woman, searching her eyes and her soul for any kind of answer.

"What kind of a person does that make me?"

The bus rolled to a stop and the woman carried her son toward the exit. She looked back at Cathy one last time before stepping off. The bus doors closed and the lights flickered and Cathy became the sole passenger.

The bus driver looked in his rear view mirror and yelled back, "hey lady, where's your stop?"

Cathy looked up and found the bus driver's eyes in the mirror. She looked down at her guitar case, then shook her head and stared out the window.

"I don't have one."

The bus idled for a moment before the air brakes lifted. The driver put the bus back into gear and disappeared into the San Fernando Valley night.

CHAPTER 25

In the flared light of morning, a man in a hard hat peered over the lip of a Florida sinkhole with a pair of Bushnell binoculars pointed downward into the abyss. "HEY REGGIE! WE GOT A FUCKING BODY DOWN HERE!"

Sam Stone's eyes slowly peeled opened. He stared back at the man in the hard hat one hundred feet above him. He immediately recognized the man and his binoculars. It was Rich, Cathy's ex, who worked for the power company, and also the Crab Castle.

Sam couldn't speak and he wasn't sure if he was alive, dreaming, or in some sort of purgatory. He lay flat on his back, surrounded by dirt, drywall, shingles, cinderblocks, and wood. Directly underneath him lay the completely uprooted banana tree from his backyard—its broken branches and leaves had provided the miraculous cushion that had stopped his fall. He could feel his legs, but he was too afraid to move them. His back was surely broken.

A second hard hat peered over the edge of the sinkhole.

"Hey, I think I fuckin' know this guy," Rich commented to Reggie, handing him his prized binoculars. Reggie peered through them and found Sam through the optics. "Holy shit, man. Hey, are you alive?!" Reggie yelled into the pit.

#

What felt like an eternity later, a crane lowered Reggie and a medic into the sinkhole to retrieve Sam. As they strapped him onto a wooden board and secured his neck in a brace, Sam somehow spotted his John Prine record embedded in the wall of the sinkhole, it's corner lodged in the black soil.

"Can you grab that?" Sam asked.

Reggie spotted the record and looked at Sam like he was crazy. "Forget it, man. You know how lucky you are?"

"Please, it was my grandfather's," Sam begged through clenched teeth, the taste of his own blood filling his mouth. As the crane lifted them up past the record, Reggie snatched it from the sinkhole. Its vinyl was somehow still encased in the cardboard sleeve. He placed the record on Sam's chest. Sam clutched the album to his body before promptly losing consciousness.

#

Sam awoke in a corner room on the fourth floor of Escapade Municipal Hospital with pain shooting through every nerve ending in his body. He squinted down the bridge of his nose to discover that his legs were in a double cast and his midsection was wrapped. He couldn't move his head at all, it was encased in one of those metal spider contraptions that hospitals use on broken necks. He was completely immobile. Sam could hear a TV on the right side of the room, but he couldn't turn his head to see it.

A door opened and someone entered the room. Sam couldn't see who it was, but he heard the unmistakable sound of someone changing out a trash bag.

"Sorry, I'm just changing this. I'll be out of your hair in a minute," a very familiar voice called out. Sam couldn't quite place it, but he was glad his ears were working.

"Stone?" the voice called out again. Sam recognized the voice as clear as day now, but it couldn't be, could it? More footsteps, and then Dan, his old boss, stood by his bed. He was dressed in blue scrubs with a hair net to complete the ensemble.

"What the hell happened to you?" Dan asked.

Sam's jaw was wired shut, but he managed to mutter, "My house tried to kill me."

"Well if you're house hadn't tried, I was going to. You cost me four grand on that Gutierrez marker, you know that, right?"

"I'm sorry, Dan," Sam mumbled. He meant it, and Dan could tell. Dan just shook his head and stared at Sam in his sorry state. Sam stared back at Dan in his hospital getup and convinced himself that he had awoken in some sort of alternate universe.

"What are you doing here?" Sam asked.

"I volunteer here four times a week, usually in the mornings," Dan replied. "Did I never tell you that?"

Sam suddenly felt like an asshole for judging Dan all those times he saw him leave work in the middle of the day.

"No," Sam replied.

The door clunked open and a nurse wheeled in a fresh IV bag. Dan picked up his trash bags. "I got more rooms to do. I'll check back on you later."

"Okay," Sam said, still convinced none of this shit was really happening. Dan made his exit as the nurse changed Sam's IV bag and pressed a few buttons on a machine. Drip. Drip. Drip.

"I'm going to raise your bed up slightly, okay?"

"Okay," Sam replied.

The nurse pressed more buttons and Sam's entire bed elevated. "Lunch will be coming in about half an hour," she said.

"Great, I was just thinking about how hungry I am," Sam said, his jaw suddenly hit with a sharp pain.

"This medicine will kick in pretty quick," the nurse reassured him. She jotted something on his chart and spotted the dirt-speckled John Prine record sitting on the table next to his bed. She picked it up and examined the cover.

"What is this, hillbilly music?" she joked, lifting the record up so Sam could see it.

"I don't know," Sam said. "I've never heard it."

"You know, we have a small record player in the lounge. I could bring it in here if you wanted to listen to it."

Sam's eyes lit up. "Okay," he said.

Five minutes of silence passed and then the nurse brought in the record player and plugged it into the wall socket next to Sam's bed. Sam watched as she slid the vinyl out of the sleeve and placed it delicately on the turntable.

"I used to be a surgeon, you know," he said.

"The medicine makes us feel a lot of things, doesn't it?" the nurse joked. She laid the record cover on Sam's chest so he could look at it.

"I recently found out I'm a father," Sam mumbled. "It's the best feeling in the world."

The nurse picked up the stylus, carried it across the grooves and laid it down on the spinning record. "Well then, congratulations are in order."

The nurse left the room and the record crackled to life. Sam lifted the record cover from his chest with his only useable hand. He made eye contact with the man on the front who stared back from all of those bales of hay.

A single acoustic guitar filled the room, and then a creaky voice. John Prine began to sing *Illegal Smile* and Sam Stone began to cry.

THE END